HARLEQUIN®
Presents

Welcome to the new collection of Harlequin Presents!

Don't miss contributions from favorite authors Michelle Reid, Kim Lawrence and Susan Napier, as well as the second part of Jane Porter's THE DESERT KINGS series, Lucy Gordon's passionate Italian, Chantelle Shaw's Tuscan tycoon and Jennie Lucas's sexy Spaniard! And look out for Trish Wylie's brilliant debut Presents book, *Her Bedroom Surrender!*

We'd love to hear what you think about Harlequin Presents. E-mail us at Presents@hmb.co.uk or join in the discussions at www.iheartpresents.com and www.sensationalromance.blogspot.com, where you'll also find more information about books and authors!

What do you look for in a guy? Charisma. Sex appeal. Confidence. A body to die for. Looks that stand out from the crowd. Well, look no further. In this brand-new collection from Harlequin Promotional Presents, you've just found six guys with all this—and more! And now that they've met the women in these novels, there is one thing on everyone's mind....

NIGHTS *of* PASSION

One night is never enough!

The guys know what they want and how they're going to get it!

Don't miss any of these hot stories where sparky romance and sizzling passion are guaranteed!

Look out for more NIGHTS OF PASSION in *His Mistress by Arrangement* by Natalie Anderson, available next month in Harlequin Presents!

Trish Wylie

HER BEDROOM SURRENDER

NIGHTS *of* PASSION

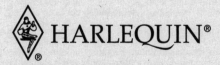

HARLEQUIN®

TORONTO • NEW YORK • LONDON
AMSTERDAM • PARIS • SYDNEY • HAMBURG
STOCKHOLM • ATHENS • TOKYO • MILAN • MADRID
PRAGUE • WARSAW • BUDAPEST • AUCKLAND

If you purchased this book without a cover you should be aware
that this book is stolen property. It was reported as "unsold and
destroyed" to the publisher, and neither the author nor the
publisher has received any payment for this "stripped book."

ISBN-13: 978-0-373-12730-6
ISBN-10:   0-373-12730-8

HER BEDROOM SURRENDER

First North American Publication 2008.

Previously published in the U.K. under the title BREATHLESS!

Copyright © 2007 by Trish Wylie.

All rights reserved. Except for use in any review, the reproduction or
utilization of this work in whole or in part in any form by any electronic,
mechanical or other means, now known or hereafter invented, including
xerography, photocopying and recording, or in any information storage
or retrieval system, is forbidden without the written permission of the
publisher, Harlequin Enterprises Limited, 225 Duncan Mill Road,
Don Mills, Ontario, Canada M3B 3K9.

This is a work of fiction. Names, characters, places and incidents are
either the product of the author's imagination or are used fictitiously,
and any resemblance to actual persons, living or dead, business
establishments, events or locales is entirely coincidental.

This edition published by arrangement with Harlequin Books S.A.

® and TM are trademarks of the publisher. Trademarks indicated with
® are registered in the United States Patent and Trademark Office, the
Canadian Trade Marks Office and in other countries.

www.eHarlequin.com

Printed in U.S.A.

All about the author...
Trish Wylie

TRISH WYLIE tried various careers before
eventually fulfilling her dream of writing. Years spent
working in the music industry, in promotions, and
teaching little kids about ponies gave her plenty of
opportunity to study life and the people around her—
Which in Trish's opinion is a pretty good study course
for writing! Living in Ireland, Trish balances her time
between writing and horses. If you get to spend
your days doing things you love, then she thinks that's
not doing too badly. You can contact her at
www.trishwylie.com.

If you can't wait for Trish's next Harlequin
Presents, be sure to look out for her book,
The Millionaire's Proposal
in Harlequin Romance September 2008....

CHAPTER ONE

'WHAT CAN I do for you?'

Cara stared up into the darkest eyes she had ever seen while her subconscious mind formed an X-rated list of answers to that particular question.

He had the eyes of a devil. Midnight-black, but with sharp sparks of light, like diamonds sprinkled on a coalface. And that voice! A deep baritone grumble that sent tremors through the air, ripples that washed over her body and called out to every pheromone she possessed. Men like him weren't supposed to exist.

He hadn't been there before. Had he? Oh, no, she'd have remembered if she'd seen him before. And the sight of him now made her falter.

'Erm, hi.'

She scowled briefly, compensating for her pathetic lack of eloquence in the sight of such potent male sexuality by running right on in with, 'I'm Cara Sheehan and I need help losing some weight.'

Great. Well, that would impress him no end. Just as well she hadn't come in here looking for anything other than some professional assistance, wasn't it? Fighting down the fact that she felt like someone who'd just stood up and confessed a deeply held secret at some kind of Over-Eaters Anonymous meeting, she focused intently on the man in front of her.

If he'd been behind the counter any of the half dozen times she'd walked past the gym doors in the last two weeks she might have come in sooner. Or never come in at all. *He'd* have got her attention much faster than weights and cycling machines. Oh yes. No doubts there.

And no doubt he didn't have any difficulty whatsoever getting women to babble incoherently at him. Which made her feel marginally better for succumbing herself.

With a swipe of her tongue over dry lips she added for good measure, 'Er, quite *fast,* as it happens.'

'We don't do any fad diets here.'

Struggling against the warmth that rose in her cheeks, she tilted her chin up and searched his dark eyes. The man could make a fortune playing poker. He didn't even flinch. He just looked straight back at her and waited. Silently.

He had no way of knowing how she made her living. Someone like him would have absolutely no need to know who the best-selling author of what some might have deemed 'fad' diet books in Ireland was. Or that she was standing in front of him right that second.

Not that there was much physical evidence that she could practise what she preached.

She raised her chin a defensive inch anyway, just for good measure. 'If I wanted something that quick, I'd have paid for liposuction. I'm prepared to put in the time.'

'And effort.'

'Yes, and effort.' She folded her arms defensively beneath her ample breasts and watched as his gaze dropped in that direction. So she unfolded them again. She hadn't done it to get his attention. And she hated men who ended up holding a conversation with them.

Mind you. It had been a while since somebody had looked at them and made them tingle the way they were right that minute. Silently, Cara prayed that her nipples wouldn't stand to attention as if it were a cold day outside. Instead, she thought about liposuction to distract herself. Which, in a moment of desperation, she *had* actually considered. But she was fairly sure it would hurt. And she had a very low pain threshold.

His dark eyes lowered and swept over her body in a cursory, yet all-encompassing gaze. Which made her suck in her stomach a little. Never before had she felt so on display, so self-conscious. So lacking in the tools needed to allow her to hold herself with more confidence in her own powers of attraction.

These were all feelings she should really have been used to by now. But under the sensual invasion of her senses by a man like this one, well…

Clearing her throat in annoyance, she smiled a small, sarcastic smile when his gaze rose to lock with hers again, 'Maybe I should just strip down to my underwear so you could study me better.'

There was a spark in his eyes, 'Up to you. But don't let me stop you.'

Arrogance had never actually done anything much for Cara. *Before*.

'I'd like to speak to someone who thinks with their brain if that's at all possible. Your *boss* maybe.'

His broad shoulders shrugged beneath his form fitting T-shirt, briefly wrinkling the dark material across his chest and tightening the sleeves around the muscles in his upper arms. He looked as if *he* had no problem keeping his weight right. Maybe he was in stage one of the steroid game and was trying to make himself into the Neanderthal man he was behaving like? He was certainly in the right place.

The fact that her body was responding to the blatant masculinity didn't help her mood any though. Damned traitorous hormones.

'I *am* the boss.'

He just would be, wouldn't he? Terrific. It had taken her nearly two weeks to summon up the motivation to walk through the glass doors and now she had *him* to contend with. Someone, somewhere really hated her, didn't they?

'Well, if this is how you encourage new business, you may as well put the For Sale sign up now.' She spun on her heel with her chin still held high. There were other gyms in the city; she didn't need to attend this one.

Even if it was the closest one to home. Though choosing the closest one to home probably didn't bode well for her determination to get out and widen her horizons more. One further away would have invited her to make more of an effort to begin with, right?

So much for step one of her great plan.

'Wait a minute.'

The deep voice sounded firmly behind her. And even though a part of her, the *sensible* part, wanted to march on out the doorway on a wave of righteous indignation, she stopped. Sighing loudly, she turned around to look at him again.

He had come out from behind the large counter, the entire length of his body now open to her perusal. And he really did fill the eye, didn't he?

Easily over six feet tall, six one or two at a stretch, with thick, lustrous dark hair that fell in errant wisps across a forehead currently wrinkled with a frown. Thick dark brows, folded over the dense lashes that framed those amazing eyes. A nose that looked as if it had maybe been broken at some point, which made him vaguely more human. And a mouth that had creases on either side that suggested he did actually smile sometimes, not that Cara had seen any evidence of it so far.

Oh, he was easy on the eyes all right, but he also had an air of surliness about him. Which made the fact that she was so viscerally affected by him all the harder to take.

It was only as he made another step or two in her direction that she was distracted from his face and eyes long enough to notice the cause of his frown.

He was limping. Distinctly. Which meant at least part of his grimace had to be related to pain.

As her blue eyes dropped down long, jean-clad legs she even expected to see a cast. Nope; just huge feet in equally huge boots.

But even though the sight of a human being in pain should have garnered *some* sympathy, Cara's mouth, as usual, had different ideas. She glanced back up as he got closer.

'Last potential customer kick you in the shins, did she?'

He stopped and his thick brows rose, a quizzical expression on his face. 'What?'

'Last person you were rude to. Did they kick you? Run you over in their car as they made an escape? Have a big stick with them?'

Dark eyes blinked across at her. And then the creases around his mouth deepened as he smiled a disgustingly sexy smile. 'Not quite.'

Cara thought about folding her arms again and then decided against it. Nope. He'd looked enough already, 'Well you needn't think your being lame is gonna get you any sympathy.'

'I wouldn't thank you for sympathy.'

'Well, it's just as well I'm not offering any then, isn't it?'

He stepped closer, the confident smile still in place. Then he stretched a large hand in her direction, his eyes narrowing a barely perceptible amount when she almost stepped back from him. 'Shall we try starting over?'

'Is that an attempt at an apology for being so bad at customer service?'

'We may have got off on the wrong foot.'

'Ooh, meaning you're less of a moron when you stand on the one you're not lame on?'

The smile faded, the frown reappeared, and the proffered hand dropped back to his side. 'Do you want my help or not? Not that I think you need it.'

Cara snorted. 'Yeah, right. Is your guide dog behind the counter?'

'Nope. I can see just fine, thanks. There's nothing wrong with a few curves. Too many women are obsessed with looking like a broom handle these days and that's not what we do here.'

She gaped up at him while he spoke. 'Jeez, you must make a clean fortune from this place when you encourage people to join like this. Next you'll be telling me that half the planet doesn't think that women who have to jump round in the shower to get wet are sexier.'

She regretted using the word 'sexier' the minute it left her lips.

The fact that her brain had thought to say the word in a lower tone, accompanied by a coquettish tilt of her chin and a suggestive batting of long eyelashes, probably hadn't helped, either.

Damn her stupid mouth.

His eyes seemed to darken a shade, if that was possible, and he quirked a single eyebrow at her, his deep voice lowering. 'Some of us find curves much—' his eyes swept down over her body and back up again as he rumbled '—sexier.'

Cara gaped more visibly as her pulse beat erratically. Oh, this guy just wasn't for real, was he? Mind you, as insane as he would appear to be, his blatant testosterone was reaching across the small gap between them and doing things to her hormone levels that had really never, ever, been done before.

And how was that fair?

Because it wasn't as if a guy like him would even take the time to look at her. Not beyond a businesslike, 'this woman is a client who needs to lose weight' way.

No man who looked like him, with that confident air and oozing sensuality about him, had ever looked her way. And if by some miracle he had, there would have been no point. Because even a few nights of mutually pleasurable, wanton passion were beyond her capabilities. No matter how much she craved them.

Not that she wouldn't enjoy taking a little of the self-control from him, given the opportunity. Lord knew her self-confidence could do with a rocket boost like that.

But that was fantasy. And Cara was a realist.

So she did the one thing she could do. She stared at him. Allowed herself to savour him with her eyes in the same way she would have to with cake and ice cream for the foreseeable future.

But then Cara Sheehan had never been famous for her good taste in men, or her timing, or her ability to detect mental instability. Though she might possibly be getting better with the latter.

'You're the kind of nut job that gets a real kick out of the fact there's fresh meat through these doors every day, aren't you?'

'Actually I'm not here every day.'

'That explains why you're still in business.' She tilted her head the other way and smiled sarcastically again.

'Are you always this friendly when someone tries to be nice to you?'

'Is that what you're doing?'

The material of his T-shirt strained as he moved his arms behind his back and shrugged again, drawing Cara's eyes to the large number sixty-nine printed there.

A subliminal message of sorts?

She swallowed hard. *Behave, Cara.* She forced herself to look back into his eyes as he spoke.

'That was the general idea, yeah. I will admit I may be a tad rusty, though. I've been out of the country for a while and I'm not used to making small talk. So you'll have to excuse me for that.'

'Avoiding someone's husband, I suppose.'

Oh, Cara, just shut up! Why was it she never knew when to stay quiet? It was a knee-jerk reaction of old and she knew it. But really, at twenty-seven she should have some sense of control by now. Lord knew it wasn't as if it hadn't caused her plenty of heartache before.

He changed stance and folded his arms across his chest again. And Cara found herself doing exactly what she had so recently mentally berated him for doing. She stared at his chest. At the suggestive number that had grown smaller as the material moved. At the way the muscles were defined in his upper arms, and the steady rise and fall of his crossed forearms as he breathed in and out.

She felt another rush of warmth spread over her body as she watched. She really needed to get out of the house more, didn't she?

A burst of deep male laughter jolted her out of her reverie. It was a completely unexpected sound, way too joyous to have come from the sullen man in front of her. So she blinked as she glanced around to see where it had come from, until her eyes once again locked with darkly sparkling ones.

'Are you always this defensive, Miss Sheehan?'

Hell, yes, as it happened. And her overly sarcastic nature had always got her in trouble. But then she had due cause to be that way. If he'd lived in her shoes for the last five years, hell, longer than that, then he'd have learned the art of verbal self-defence, too. It was a survival thing.

But she wasn't about to explain that to a complete stranger. No matter how tempting he was in the most basic of ways otherwise. So she lifted her chin instead and dared him to laugh at her again.

Go on. Make my day.

After a moment he dropped his chin, clearing his throat as he brought his smile under control before he glanced at her with hooded 'come to bed' eyes. But the smile was still twitching at the edges of his mouth as he unfolded his arms and reached a hand out again.

'I promise to behave if you do. C'mon. Who knows what we might get out of it?'

Ignoring the way his voice had dropped to a deep grumble on the suggestion, Cara looked down at the proffered hand. It was a very large hand. A very masculine hand. With long fingers that looked as if they would have the ability to circle her wrist and hold on no matter how much she tried to shake free. A part of her felt intimidated by that thought, while another part, a more secret, well-buried part, was immediately, ragingly turned on by it.

'I didn't come in here to make some kind of pact with the devil.'

'No, you came in here to tone up some. I can help you do that—' his mouth twitched again '—even if I don't think you need it.'

Well she did. She really did. And not just for her sense of self-esteem or as step one of the great plan. There was yet another emotional mountain to be climbed soon and this time, for once, she wanted to face it with all the equipment at hand she could muster. And that meant she needed help. Because she hadn't got to be the chubby one of her group of friends overnight and she'd be damned if she let one more person—

Well, suffice it to say she really needed to look better than she did right that minute, no matter what this man thought.

'Isn't there anyone else?' She clutched at a straw and mentally pleaded that there would be. Even a female version of Attila the Hun would be preferable to this guy with his oozing testosterone and sparkling eyes. In fact, Attila was exactly the kind of taskmaster she needed.

Cara had been a professional yo-yo dieter for most of her life, after all. If she was going to work away the damage of half a lifetime, then she really didn't need any distractions. Or anything that might send her running to the fridge to compensate for other sensual rewards she couldn't have.

'My brother is on holiday for a while, so that makes me the best there is.'

'Meaning there's actually someone better than you?'

His eyes sparkled all the more. 'At some things.'

Cara held her palm in front of his face and wiggled her fingers. 'Bye-bye.'

But as she turned he did what she'd been thinking about only moments before. As if he'd read her mind. His hand shot forwards. Long fingers encircled her wrist, curling over her skin, holding her in place. Dominating her with sheer masculine strength.

And Cara burned where he touched. As if she'd spent a full day in the sun without lotion. Only this heat was under her skin, inside her veins, pulsing in her blood. She stared down at the contact in stark surprise.

What the hell was *that*?

He stepped closer, his voice dropping to a tone that spoke of early mornings, tangled up sheets and naked, soon-to-be-sated bodies. 'If I let you walk out that door, my brother will throw a fit. Probably even kick me in my bad leg. You wouldn't want that on your conscience now would you, *Cara*?'

Actually Cara was fairly sure she wouldn't have a problem with that at all. But the next one got her.

'And I get results. Every time. Sarcasm doesn't phase me, being stubborn doesn't work with me, and motivation is my middle name. So if you really want to work at this, then I'm your man. If you think you can deal with me, that is.'

The suggestion hung in the air between them as he brushed a calloused thumb back and forth over the pulse that was beating erratically in her wrist. Dealing with him would certainly be the bigger issue. But he had listed all the things he would have to cope with working with her and he had her at the getting results part. Because that was all she was really interested in.

She couldn't go through yet another wedding as the fat bridesmaid, the one that everyone said had such a pretty face—a double-edged compliment for anyone who carried extra weight. Yes, it was nice to know you had a pretty face, but it always came across as something they said in order to find something nice to say when all else failed.

And Cara just couldn't do it to herself again.

Just one time, she wanted them all to be blown away by how she looked instead of feeling sorry for her. She wanted them to see that she was in control of her life, confident, happy with herself. Even though she was alone. Added to that, the fact that Niall would see her and realize she was actually better off without him was too good a bonus to miss.

It was an all-round golden opportunity.

Dealing with this clown would be a short-term deal. That was all. Needs must and all that.

'So.' She twisted gently but firmly to free her wrist, accompanying it with a determined gaze, and was both surprised and possibly even a little disappointed when he set her free without a fight. Then she straightened her shoulders, subconsciously communicating to him he didn't intimidate her, and quirked a brow at him. 'That means I get a refund if you don't get the results, then, does it?'

The lopsided smile reappeared and he winked. 'I've never disappointed a woman so far.'

Terrific. So long as he kept coming out with that kind of macho crap she would have absolutely no problem dealing with him.

So with a smirk she nodded. 'First time for everything, hop-a-long.'

'Rory.'

She blinked at him.

'It's my name. Rory Flanaghan. I know you'll have been wondering. And you'll need a name for the doll you're gonna stick pins in this next while.'

'Well, Rory Flanaghan. You'd better be as good as you say you are.'

With only a moment's hesitation he leaned closer and whispered, 'I thought we were going to behave.'

There was a distinct pause before she answered him.

'I want the refund part in writing.'

CHAPTER TWO

CARA JUMPED. DAMN, but the man had electric hands!

'Watch it, big guy.'

He blinked at her. 'I'm just putting you in the right position.'

She couldn't help herself, eyes twinkling and the corners of her mouth lifting as she replied, 'I bet you say that to all the girls.'

A low rumble of laughter escaped his mouth as he continued using the flat of his hand to encourage her to straighten her spine. 'Now Cara, if you're going to start flirting with me, I'm going to have to stop behaving—your call. But you wouldn't want me to end up looking like some kind of sleaze, would you? Ruin my good reputation as a personal trainer and all…'

She frowned as her upper arms protested at another use of muscles that hadn't been used, well, probably ever. If she was flirting, it wasn't intentional. Really it wasn't. And even if she'd wanted to, it wouldn't have done her any good. Not judging by the number of stick-thin women who had all batted their lashes at him since she'd started at the gym. He was a popular guy.

Though, to be fair, he hadn't played up to any of them. Not that Cara had seen anyway. Which earned him a few Brownie points.

'I'm not flirting, I'm being witty. I'm great at witty. Just down my list from sarcasm and comfort eating. I'm *fantastic* at both of those.'

Rory lifted his hand from her back when he was sure she

wasn't rounding her spine, his eyes focused on the arms of the weights apparatus. 'What else are you *fantastic* at?'

Cara looked at him from the corner of her eye. 'Thought you didn't want to come across like some kinda sleaze? That question will help no end.'

'That wasn't what I meant.'

'Course it wasn't.'

Dark eyes focused on her face again as he reached an arm out and leaned against the side of the apparatus, a smile twitching on the edges of his mouth as he tilted his face closer. 'Maybe I was making conversation.'

'Then why don't you just ask me about the weather?'

'Because I can see the weather through the front doors if I want to.'

'World peace, then? The environment? Whether or not there'll be holidays in space before we die?'

'Two more here and we'll move on.' He glanced briefly at her arms again and took a breath. 'Don't you ever have a normal conversation? Simple question followed by simple answer kind of thing? Most men find that easier to keep up with.'

Cara smiled at that. As much for the fact that Rory Flanaghan was the least like 'most men' she had ever met. But he had a point about the conversation thing. 'Most men are simple? Is that what you're saying?'

Dark eyes sparkled in amusement. 'Time to move on.'

Letting go of the weighted arms that then clunked metal off metal, Cara stood up, falling into step beside him as they moved to the treadmill. She watched from the corner of her eye as he glanced around the room, taking in what everyone was doing with one all encompassing glance before he looked back at her.

Was it any bit of wonder she spent so much time trying to stay ahead of him in conversation? It was the only thing she seemed to have any modicum of control over in his presence. Even walking the few steps it took to get from one piece of equipment to the other became some kind of test on her senses.

He was so annoyingly self-contained and professional all the time, she wanted to scream. How could he have such a physical effect on her and not notice? Mind you, his noticing her reaction to him would be bad with a capital *B*.

Maybe he was just used to it.

Women probably swarmed round him like flies round—

'We'll do twenty minutes on this one today.'

Cara watched as he pushed the settings on the treadmill. 'I just love the way you say that like you're actually doing this with me. I'm the one doing the walking. You just stand there.'

'And watch what you're doing.'

Uh-huh. And therein lay the problem. Cara spent just as much energy trying to stay tall, shoulders back and with her stomach sucked in to her spine, as she did on the actual exercises. Which, granted, probably meant she was getting twice the workout, but even so…

'Would it make you feel better if I walked at the same time?' He patted the rail of the machine beside hers.

She pursed her mouth, using his invitation as an excuse to look down his long legs. Her eyes lingered longer than necessary on the drawstring of his dark sweat pants, skimmed very quickly past the loose material below it and then down to his large trainer-clad feet.

And she swallowed hard before she glanced back up. To find his eyes glinting and his dark eyebrows raised.

'You can hardly go walking on a treadmill with that leg, can you?'

'I'm not in a wheelchair just yet.' He leaned back over the rail and punched some keys. 'I'll just take it nice and easy while you walk uphill.'

'And they say chivalry is dead.'

They stepped onto the machines at the same time. And Cara did her best not to look at him as she let her step fall into a rhythm. But she still knew he was there; could still see his dark head out of her peripheral vision, was conscious of his steady pace and the large hand that was resting on the rail close to hers.

She couldn't ever remember being so conscious of someone's presence before. Or their scent. And he smelled *great*. Every time he would lean past her to adjust something or they would walk by an open window, his scent would reach across and surround her. So very male, with a base tone of cinnamon, she thought, and she knew it would always remind her of him if she smelled it again.

It still bugged the hell out of her that she noticed things like that. Surely the novelty should have worn off after a day or two? *C'mon!*

Finally his deep voice grumbled alongside her, 'I'm pro-rain-forest myself.'

Cara smiled a small smile as she continued looking ahead. 'Me, too.'

'And world peace *would* be nice.'

'Yeah, I think so.'

They walked a while longer, then his voice sounded again. 'And every guy would like to say he sent a woman to the moon and back.'

She laughed aloud and turned her head to look at him at the same time as he winked at her with a wicked grin. He just couldn't help himself, could he?

It was actually quite charming in a mischievous teenager kinda way. The kind of teenager whose mother had probably regularly cuffed him around the ear for giving her cheek and laughed while she did it.

Cara frowned as she focused forwards again.

Oh, no.

She was *so* not going to start to *like* him. To find his sense of humour charming! He was the kind of guy a gal's mother warned her about; the kind that would have you charmed horizontal before you realized your feet weren't on the ground any more. *Nope.*

And it would be pretty pointless. All she would have to do was look around and she'd bet there were at least three potential candidates behind her waiting for his charm to be bestowed on them for an hour each day, on varying pieces of gym equipment.

Cara had never been the first girl to be picked from a line-up for *any* kind of sport, so what would be the point in playing along?

Yep. It was one thing being uncontrollably physically aware of someone who looked like he did; entirely another finding him *charming* in a roguish kind of way.

And way into the realms of move-to-another-country embarrassing if he ever found out she felt either one.

It would probably have the same effect on him as finding out that King Kong loved her did to the blonde on the big tower in the movie.

Cara took a deep breath. Sarcasm was called for. 'Just so long as she didn't take the trip there to get away from him, huh?'

With a small smirk sideways for good measure, she focused her gaze forwards again, feeling the burn in the front of her legs as the angle of the treadmill increased; welcoming it in fact. She'd walk up Everest at this point if it meant she could forget for a moment that he was right beside her. Being so *likeable!*

'Are you this uppity with everyone, or are you just singling me out 'cos I'm making you work out?'

Uppity? She glanced across at him again in amusement. 'Did y'all tie up your horse outside when you mosey-ed in here this morning?'

Her bad attempt at an American cowgirl accent drew another rumble of laughter from him. 'Very funny.'

'I'm good at funny.' She looked forwards again and raised her chin. 'It's just down the list of things I'm good at from being liked by small children and animals and keeping smart-mouthed personal trainers in their place.'

'You really hate working out, don't you?'

She sighed in defeat. 'Yes, I do.'

'Then why put yourself through it?'

Another sideways glance. 'And again I'm going to ask where you keep your guide-dog?'

'You do that a lot.' He hit a key on his treadmill and turned to face her when it stopped, leaning back against the rail and folding his arms across his broad chest, 'Is putting yourself down a hobby of some kind? Or are you one of those women who does it to get compliments?'

Cara snorted gracefully in reply. 'Yeah, right.'

'Well, I don't see what the problem is. You're obviously intelligent, a bit of a comedienne all right, but you're pro-rainforest and vote for world peace; it's all good from where I'm standing.'

It didn't escape her notice that he hadn't listed a single good physical attribute in his list. Not even the pretty face that was her usual back-up. And she hated that she felt a pang of disappointment at that. It wasn't as if she wanted him to find her fanciable in the first place after all, was it?

'Okay. I just said something bad there, obviously.'

Cara shook her head, eyes forward.

There was a lengthy pause to her right. Then a deep breath she could hear over the machine, 'So if you don't like working out and you're not interested in making simple conversation without trying to keep me in my place, what exactly can we talk about for an hour a day?'

'Do we *have* to talk?'

'It's a bit boring if we don't.'

'Couldn't you just see it as an opportunity to pretend you're a librarian?'

There was another low chuckle of laughter. 'Not something I've ever felt like doing, to be honest.'

'Well it's not like we have anything in common to talk about, is it?'

'You don't know that.' He unfolded his arms and stepped down, walking round to lean in front of her and adjust the angle of the treadmill so she was walking up a steeper hill. Then he looked up at her from beneath thick lashes, studying her for several heartbeats. 'We already have shared beliefs in world peace and rainforests, that's a place to start.'

Cara swallowed hard, again. His scent filling her nostrils, again. The thud of her heart having absolutely nothing to do with the steep climb she was currently making. Again.

'Is it really necessary that you know my thoughts on life, the universe and everything? All you need to do is make sure I don't break my neck on any of these instruments of torture, so I don't sue.'

'Maybe I'd just like to know.'

Oh, man, he was *good*. He'd managed to say that with just the right amount of softness in his eyes and intimacy in his voice. As if he genuinely gave two figs.

The treadmill began to slow.

Rory continued to look up at her with those dark eyes, waiting for her to answer him.

Cara ran the tip of her tongue across her lips and watched as he followed the movement.

'Are you this much of a pain in the butt with all your clients?'

He smiled a slow smile. 'No. I told you, I'm not here that much.'

'Well, it's not like you're short of candidates who'd like for you to get to know them better.' She tilted her head a little, her voice dropping. 'Maybe you should just put the effort in with them and let me be the one to bring you back down to earth for an hour a day.'

'I've never been one for the easy life.'

Cara rolled her eyes.

And he chuckled again in reply. 'We'll be able to work together a lot better when you admit I'm not half as bad as you like to think I am.'

'I have no actual proof of that.'

'Well, then, you just need to get to know me better, don't you?'

Had he just talked her round in a circle to his way of thinking? Cara frowned as she thought about it. Yes, he had. Damn it.

He was *good*.

'No stalking me.'

'Cross my heart.' He crossed the region of his heart with one long finger, a smile twitching on his lips and sparkling in the dark depths of his eyes.

As the machine stopped Cara waggled her forefinger in warning, 'No thinking that I'll let you get away with those monstrous one liners of yours that probably work on other women.'

'I think that's a given.' The hint of a smile transformed into a fully fledged, killer grin.

And Cara found herself smiling back before she lifted one brow in warning. 'And definitely none of *that*.'

Rory chuckled. 'Now that I can't guarantee.'

Cara shook her head as she turned round and stepped off the treadmill, her eyes rising to meet his when she was back to her normal height. 'Well, just so you know it's not going to get you anywhere.'

'So long as *you* know—' his palm settled on the small of her back again as he steered her to the next exercise, leaning his head down to stage whisper '—that that just came out as a challenge.'

If he had any idea *how much* of a challenge he might just give up; for once.

Cara sighed inwardly. In another life and with the body of a supermodel, that little battle might have been one hell of a lot of fun.

CHAPTER THREE

'YOU HAVE A very extensive vocabulary for someone who otherwise looks so sweet and innocent, you know.'

Rory swallowed back a smile as Cara glared up at him, her face flushed and damp with exertion. Long tendrils of her deep brown shoulder-length hair had escaped from their loose plaits and plastered to her cheeks. And every time he insisted she manage another sit-up or another five minutes on an exercise bike, she would grit her teeth and swear at him. Like a trooper.

'I'll bet—' she forced her pelvis upwards as she pressed her heels into the Swiss Ball '—women call you names—' held the position for a second before lowering with a flop to the floor '—all the damn time.'

He did his best not to watch the upward and downward movement of her pelvis. That would be unprofessional, wouldn't it? In fact, after twenty minutes of watching her in varying thrusts and bends over the ball, he was fairly sure he was past unprofessional and bordering on being a pervert. Just what was it about this woman?

Ever since she had walked in through the door and looked up at him with those Pacific-Ocean-blue eyes of hers, he had had but one thought in his head. And its name was Cara Sheehan.

She had a way of looking at him that made him feel like some kind of illicit treat she couldn't allow herself to have. Which was sexy as all hell.

And she was sharp as a tack mentally, which kept him on his toes, their verbal bantering helping to distract him from *other* things.

In theory.

He cleared his throat. 'Not with quite so much colour in the terminology, no.'

Her blue eyes narrowed as she looked at him from the corner of her eye. 'You look that word up in the dictionary today, did you?'

'It was word of the day in the paper.'

'The one with the naked women on the third page?'

'That's the one.' His smile escaped. 'Again. Come on, you have five of these to do before we move on.'

Five more of this, six more of that, and Rory was fairly sure she was smart enough to realize he was adding a few every time. But she didn't stop, she just gritted her teeth, called him a 'sadist' and kept going.

He liked that about her.

Nearly a week in and she was showing the same kind of gutsy determination he'd had to call on in himself since he'd come home. And he could empathize with that. It garnered his respect; helped hold hotter thoughts at bay.

She was a client after all. And if she weren't?

Well, suffice to say all prior deals would be off.

'You're doing great.'

'Don't you dare patronize me. You haven't seen me trying to crawl outta bed in the morning. I have aches in places I didn't know I had muscles.'

For days he had watched her struggle her way through the routines he had put together. For days she had been gritting her teeth and turning the air blue with her names for the varying pieces of equipment and making him laugh with her sarcastic wit. And for just as long, he had been finding it harder and harder to stay professional.

Literally and figuratively.

Yet he still had no idea why she was putting herself through it. Maybe, simply because he hadn't asked?

Well, that was easily fixed and a little conversation could help him think cooling thoughts. 'It must be some real big deal for you to be putting yourself through this. I'll lay odds that there wasn't a problem with a bikini before.'

He was just about able to get away with saying something like that since their tentative 'truce'. But he still smiled as he waited for her reply. Winding her up was one of his favourite hobbies now.

She snorted. 'Never worn one, as it happens.'

As they had so recently of late, his eyes dropped to her breasts. Oh, he'd bet she looked great in a bikini. Or out of it. There was just something about a woman who curved where a woman was supposed to curve...

He scowled. Enforced celibacy of late was obviously having a very detrimental effect on that professionalism he was struggling to hang on to. But even with that as an excuse, he should have had more control. After all he had spent years going through months of enforced celibacy. Though, before now, he had always managed to do something about it when he came home.

Not this time.

It made him feel marginally better that Cara was the only one he seemed so turned on by. At least he wasn't letching after every woman with a pulse.

There was just *something* about this one. 'Two more.'

She moaned a low, earthy moan. Which didn't help his libido any. Then she managed two more upward pushes before she slumped onto the floor with a deep, self-satisfied sigh. Which didn't help any, either.

But she was putting a real effort in. So he hunched down beside her and smiled a small smile, his voice dropping, 'You're doing great, you know. All kidding aside.'

Her face turned towards him, her lashes lifting as her blue eyes met his. For a long moment she just studied him, almost sizing him up before she answered.

Already having witnessed firsthand and frequently how quick-witted she could be, he knew it wasn't because she was taking time to think up a sarcastic answer. So more than likely she was deciding whether or not to let her guard down and *not* be sarcastic. Which meant she still didn't trust herself to be herself around him. And surely trusting him would help her to work with him?

It bugged him. And not just because he had made a promise to his brother, and to himself, that he would put a real effort into the business during his enforced stay.

Maybe the fact that he was constantly in a state of heightened awareness around her was a little too obvious? Well, that wasn't entirely his fault. If she didn't turn every action, every blue-eyed gaze, every swipe of her tongue over her full mouth, into what might or might not have been an unwitting come-on…

Still. He had to give it a try. He was a grown-up, after all. Thirty-year-old men with a certain amount of experience under their belt should be able to focus their minds elsewhere.

He could put sexual frustration and curiosity to the back of his mind. *He damn well could.*

So he turned on a simpler form of charm and allowed his smile to broaden into one of the wide grins that normally garnered faith from women and small children. 'You are, really. I know you must be starting to ache at this stage, especially if you don't do much of this kind of exercise. Give yourself some credit.'

With a small grimace, Cara pushed herself up onto an elbow, her eyes still locked on his as she tilted her head, cocked an arched eyebrow and asked, 'Really, you are patronizing me, aren't you?'

'Don't trust me much, do you?'

'Why would I?'

Rory shrugged. 'Oh, I dunno, maybe because it's yet another reason why it'll make it easier to work with me. You put so much effort into challenging me that you're tiring yourself out way more than you need to while you work out.'

'Aw.' She smiled and batted her eyelids. 'Not feeling the love, big guy?'

He laughed. Oh, she was something wasn't she? He wondered

if she knew how much of a flirt she was. She'd deny it if he asked, though, wouldn't she?

'Nope. Not so much.'

Eyes sparkling, she struggled up onto her feet while he stood and waited, knowing instinctively that a hand offered to help her up would only be rebuffed or challenged. Then he watched as she raised her hands and smoothed the damp tendrils off her cheeks with her palms before her sparkling eyes rose again to meet his.

She shook her head. 'Get used to it. I'm paying you to take my frustration out on, hop-a-long.'

He couldn't help himself, his smile changing tone as he took a step closer. 'And you're *frustrated,* are you?'

If she was, he could definitely help her out there.

The question had an immediate effect. Her blue eyes widened, her dark pupils enlarging, and to Rory's trained eye her flushed cheeks took on a deeper shade. He wasn't the only one whose libido was being affected by their daily workout time, was he?

All that physical effort, all that damp skin, all those little straining gasps. There was only one other thing it resembled in Rory's mind...

He hadn't missed any of the times she had let her eyes look over him. Had burned everywhere she had looked, in fact. It was about time she got some payback for that, even if he could only allow himself to flirt blatantly with her as punishment.

And for the first time since she'd walked through the glass doors of the gym, she was at a loss for words.

Rory couldn't help but smile at the victory.

'Don't be shy, you can tell your personal trainer anything. Hence the word *personal...*'

It took a moment for her to rise to the bait, her mouth opening and closing a couple of times while her eyes went from wide to narrow. 'I can't believe all this stuff actually works for you. You really can be the *most—*'

'Cara? Oh, my Lord, it *is* you!'

They turned in unison at the sound of the high-pitched voice behind them. But not before Rory had seen Cara's eyes widen with shock, and something more; something that changed the flush on her cheeks from awareness to embarrassment.

The stick-thin blonde leaned in and air kissed Cara above each cheek.

Rory hated women who did that.

She then leaned back, a foot away from him, and positively beamed at Cara. 'Well isn't this a hoot? What on earth are *you* doing in a gym?'

Rory turned a half-inch so he could look at Cara's reaction to the woman's obvious amusement, already having taken offence on Cara's behalf at her words. Not that she'd actually said anything that bad. He'd been wondering about that from the start himself after all.

And it wasn't really as if it were any of his business in the grander scheme of things. He knew enough about Cara already to know she wouldn't take too much nonsense from this woman before her sarcasm kicked in.

So he folded his arms across his chest while he waited. Promising himself that the second they started discussing clothes or shopping he would quit eavesdropping and find something else to do.

The colour had returned to Cara's cheeks. 'I know, it's ridiculous, isn't it? Well, you know it's Laura's—'

'Wedding. Of course. You don't want to look like a blimp in one of those lovely dresses, I'm sure. I'd be exactly the same myself. There's not much time, though. You'll need a miracle in that amount of time to get to where the others are.' She paused for breath, a small smile on her mouth as she added with a sympathetic tone, 'And of course Niall will be there, won't he? How dreadful. First time you'll have seen him since you broke up, isn't it? How embarrassing that he's the best man to your place as chief bridesmaid, too. You must have wanted to curl up in a ball and die when you found out, poor thing.'

Rory watched the conversation bounce back and forth like someone at a tennis match. It couldn't be helped really. He had learned more about Cara's mysterious motivation in thirty seconds than he had in days. A personal trainer should know these things, he felt.

Was Cara trying to win back an ex with all her physical effort? A part of him bristled at the thought that someone else would see her all heated up and horizontal, that she would make those little gasps she made when working out for someone else while doing something else.

Without thinking, he stepped closer to Cara's side.

Just in time to hear her clear her throat and answer, 'Erm, well, yes, the dresses *are* lovely…'

His eyes were drawn back to her profile in an attempt to find out where the small voice he'd just heard had come from. This wasn't the Cara he knew. Where were the sarcastic answers? Where was the challenging tilt of her chin? She looked like a church mouse.

Was she embarrassed that he was hearing all this?

'They have been designed with a very slim figure in mind, you'd have to say. It's the cut of the material, isn't it? Nothing's hidden. I swear, I'd be afraid to eat a lettuce leaf! Deirdre looks stunning in hers, I heard, as does Maggie, I'm sure. But then they've always been so sporty, haven't they? Sitting in front of a desk all day can't help you any.' The woman glanced around the room as she took a dramatically deep breath. 'I'd have tried a gym, too, in your shoes. But really, darling, you'd have been better starting a few months ago if you want to give yourself a sporting chance. You should know all this, writing those books of yours.'

Cara was a writer? Rory quirked a dark brow at that piece of information; what kind of books did she write, then? If there was any sex involved in them, then all attempts at professionalism on his behalf were going right out the window, no question about it.

He pursed his mouth in thought and examined his feet.

The blonde was a mine of information. She laughed musically as she looked Rory's way, waiting until she had his attention. 'You'd think someone that writes diet books would have a better understanding, wouldn't you? It's as well her readers can't see her all messy like this. Not a sign of glamour in a gym, is there? It would drop her right off the best-sellers list. But we all love her so for how funny she can be!'

His eyes jerked back to look at Cara's face as he stared at her with newfound respect. *Bestsellers list, really?* Well, hell, that was impressive.

Cara in turn grimaced, swallowed, took a deep breath, 'Yes, Moira, you're absolutely right, sitting in front of a desk doesn't help any—'

'Well, darling—' Moira reached out a hand and patted Cara's arm, her chin dropping as she pouted her bottom lip '—if you ever came out of the house after Niall left that would have helped, too, don't you think? All that hiding away. Is it any wonder he went in the end when you'd become such a recluse?' She paused for breath again. 'I've seen him with so many gorgeous women since you broke up, too. It's so sad that you're both so unhappy.'

Rory frowned as he stared at Cara's profile. Her friend's words were a complete contradiction to the Cara he knew from the last few days. She was feisty, smart, witty, intelligent, sexy; even when flushed with exertion. *Especially* when flushed with exertion.

To hear her friend talk, you'd think she was some kind of sad and lonely shadow of a woman. And she'd never once struck *him* as being like that. Far from it.

Cara glanced up at him, her blue eyes filled with what could only be described as anguish. And Rory felt his heart twist. So he smiled softly at her as he tried to silently communicate his thoughts.

Don't listen, Cara. This woman obviously knows nothing about you. Not the you I'm getting to know.

'I have to say I'm glad you're doing something pro-active about getting him back. A make-over is exactly what's called for to get a man's attention.'

Oh, come on. This woman was a friend of Cara's? Swallowing a sudden feeling of disappointment that the Cara he'd come to know hadn't reared her head to put the woman in her place, he cleared his throat and stood a little taller, willing his Cara to come out of hiding.

Go on, go get her, you can do it!

The blonde smiled his way again. Looked him up and down as if he were a piece of meat. And once she'd seen what she needed to, she became more blatantly sexual, tilting her hip in his direction as she spoke.

'And a personal trainer, no less! My, my, all those royalties must be starting to *flood* in. You lucky girl!'

One glance at Cara's face was enough for him. She grimaced, looked away, her jaw tight as she swallowed convulsively.

Enough was enough.

After all, he'd never set eyes on this woman before. And even if she'd seen him, she had no way of knowing what his relationship with Cara was, did she?

Rory was glad he'd rebelled about wearing the standard gym T-shirts that his brother insisted all the staff wore as he casually snaked an arm around Cara's waist. 'I don't actually work here. Not officially. I'm a friend of Cara's.'

Moira's eyes widened. 'Really?'

He met her look of disbelief with a steady gaze that dared her to challenge him. 'I have to do some gentle exercise as part of the physiotherapy for my leg, so she was sweet enough to come along and keep me company, weren't you, honey?'

Cara's face tilted up to look at his from its resting place in his armpit, her body tense against his side. She scowled for a second and he winked in return before glancing back at Moira.

'She hates the gym—' he squeezed his arm tighter, rewarded as her lush body fitted in against him '—but then she really has no need to come to a place like this. I like her curves just fine the way they are. Nothing like a woman who curves in the right places to encourage a guy to stay indoors with her.' He winked again, this time at Moira. 'If you know what I mean. So if anyone is to blame for her being a recluse these days, it would have to be me.'

Cara looked at Moira and smiled through a flush that had run out of room on her cheeks and worked its way down her throat.

While Moira looked back and forth from one of them to the other before her eyes narrowed. 'Well, I—'

'I better go get a shower, honey. It was nice to meet you Moira.'

He couldn't resist. The woman still didn't look as if she believed him, and that brought out the devil in him. She obviously liked to talk. Well, he'd damn well give her something to talk about.

And maybe next time she'd think before she embarrassed Cara in front of a virtual stranger.

So he tugged Cara round with his arm and leaned in to kiss her. It was a brief kiss, barely a touch of mouth to mouth. Merely aimed at putting a seal on the lie.

But its effect was immediate. Powerful. Potent.

Cara's lips were so soft, a taste of coffee and a hint of vanilla there, and the minute he brushed them with his firm mouth he felt the coiling in his gut, was aware of his body growing taut with anticipation for more of the same. Much more.

And all that from just one brief touch, one small taste.

He should have known it would feel like that from the reactions he had to everything else about her. *Nothing* about Cara Sheehan was simple.

But when he lifted his head to look down at her, a small scowl of confusion on her face, he knew it had been a mistake. Even with the best of intentions.

And as he walked away, he knew that he wanted to know why she had stared at him with such a look of agony written all over her face and spilling from her eyes.

What had been intended as an attempt at chivalry could well have been one of the most dangerous things he'd done in a while.

Which was saying something.

CHAPTER FOUR

'WHY *EXACTLY* DID you do that?'

Cara was standing, arms folded and eyes flashing, when he came out of the changing rooms. She was shaking inside, angrier than she'd been in a long, long time. And not just at what he'd done or the fact that he'd felt the need to do it in the first place. But because looking at him as he came out from his shower, damp tendrils of dark hair clinging to his head and wearing a black sweater that barely hid his muscular frame and highlighted his midnight eyes, she was also deeply aware of the fact she could still feel the touch of his mouth on hers.

As if he'd somehow branded her with his. *Damn it.*

'She needed shutting up and you weren't doing it.'

Well, that much she couldn't argue with. Moira Lenaghan had needed shutting up, or at the very least setting straight on her lack of subtlety, since high school, and Cara had never quite got round to doing it. Oh, she'd thought about it, at length, but she had never managed it aloud. As if the quiet teenager inside her was still clinging to a need to hold on to her friends for dear life. No matter how badly they'd grown in adulthood. Moira's lack of finesse was something they all knew about. But a friend was a friend. And everyone had their faults, right?

But it was Rory's way of shutting up that Cara had the biggest problem with. 'So you thought you'd just step in and rescue me from a woman I've been friendly with for years? What a hero.'

The sarcasm had as much effect on him as water off a duck's back. Instead, he looked her straight in the eye and answered with, 'With friends like that, you don't need enemies, do you? No wonder you hide inside your house.'

Bloody hell. Did he miss nothing?

He had no idea why it was she rarely left the house. Any more than he could have had any idea what that simple kiss of his had just done. Just when she had made the decision to actually make changes in her life, she had to go and get the personal trainer from hell.

'And who are you to tell me who I should be friendly with?' Not that Moira was top of her list of favourites, but even so. 'You've known me all of five minutes and you feel you have to step in and *save* me from my own life? Who made you responsible for the world? Mr. Big Guy who runs in at a moment's notice to save people's lives. Big whoop!'

A thunderous look crossed his face, the sparks in his eyes dying as if a cloud had come out and covered the reflected light.

'Well, you sure as hell weren't opening your mouth!' He stepped closer and lowered his face to bring home his point, his deep voice holding a steely edge. 'And what was with that, anyway? Every day you come in here you have some smart alec answer for me; you're sharp as a tack. And yet that woman wanders over to throw pretty much an insult a minute your way and you just stand there and let her. Whatever it is she has on you must be huge. What did you do, run over someone's cat?'

Her shoulders rose. '*That* wouldn't be any of your business, would it?'

And she knew she had him on that. And knew he knew, when there was a long pause before he took a deep breath and looked upwards as he exhaled. But as her chin rose in triumph he fixed her with his dark gaze, studying her intently until she wanted to squirm. But she would be damned if she'd squirm in front of him; would rot in hell before she'd show weakness of any kind in front of any man ever again.

Even one who could kiss to Olympic standards in less than five seconds.

Rory's voice calmed, the deep tone seeming to vibrate the air between them. 'All right. It's not. But that doesn't mean I don't want to know. You're a collection of contradictions, Cara, and, I have to say, that's fascinating to me. *Apparently.*'

Fascinating? Her? To someone like him? *Shut up!*

Cara knew she was smart, knew she was quick-witted—at least on paper. But she also knew she wasn't some 'fascinating' goddess who men like Rory Flanaghan found interesting. And nor would she want to be. That was a train wreck waiting to happen.

'It must've been a while since you got laid.'

Dark eyebrows shot up in surprise. 'Excuse me?'

'Well, it has to be if you find someone like me so all-fired fascinating. Are you finding your bad leg so restricting? Or maybe you just like a bit of a challenge?'

His eyes narrowed. And for a brief moment, as her gaze was drawn to the clench of his jaw, she thought he would lose his temper with her. She was certainly doing enough to provoke it. And that had always been half her problem with Niall, too, hadn't it?

And now she was comparing her 'relationship' with her damned personal trainer with that of a man she'd lived with! Great.

She sighed. It was really nothing to do with Rory after all. So, for the first time in a long while, she stepped down. 'I'm sorry. That was uncalled for.'

Uncalled for, maybe; close to the mark would be more truthful, if Rory chose to admit it to her—which he didn't feel like doing.

Pursing his mouth to give him time to think before he made things worse, he glanced over her shoulder at nothing in particular. 'You're right about it being none of my business. It isn't. I won't make the same mistake twice. From now on you can fight your own battles—' his eyes locked with hers again as he carefully measured his words '—whether you *choose* to fight them or not.'

Her eyes flared.

So he kept going. 'I guess I was just disappointed by the fact that you didn't. Because from what I've seen of you so far, that's just not you. It was one of the things I liked best about you when I met you.'

Cara had to step to the side to let him past her, and she was deeply conscious that she had disappointed him.

But he was so very far off the mark about her. Up until very recently, she hadn't been able to fight her own battles, not when it had really mattered.

The truth was that Rory was the first one who had brought her defences back up. Big time. It occurred to her that maybe it wasn't fair for him to bear the brunt of months' worth of anger and frustration. But he had brought it out of her with nothing more complicated than a wise-ass attitude and a level of self-confidence that she herself could only hope to aspire to.

And now she had disappointed him, which stung when it really shouldn't have mattered at all. Who was he to her, after all?

But she couldn't seem to stop herself from trying to make amends. 'Moira is a bad example of the kind of people I have as friends; I'll give you that. She has the subtlety of a bull in a china shop. Always has had. But the thing you need to keep in mind is that pretty much everything she said was true. Why would I put her down for that?'

She turned on her heel to look at his broad back where he had stopped a couple of steps away, her voice dropping while she continued. 'The truth is I can't go to that wedding looking like a blimp when Niall is there. Not this time.'

Rory didn't turn round. His shoulders rose and fell as he took a silent breath, and when he didn't answer Cara rolled her eye heavenwards. Why on earth had she just told him that? Why didn't she go right on ahead and demand a different trainer, for crying out loud? It wasn't as if it made any difference to him what she looked like in the sleek lavender silk creation her friend had chosen for her to wear. Or that her confidence would benefit greatly from showing the world she was better off without Niall in her life.

Rory turned around. And Cara held her breath as he blinked at her.

'First up: you don't look like a blimp, just so you know. I've already mentioned that a time or two in a roundabout way.'

She saw the opportunity for a wisecrack to ease the tension and get her off dangerous ground. But he only let her get as far as opening her mouth.

'*Secondly.* I can't be held responsible for what I might do if you let someone talk to you like that again without your usual knack for sarcasm. Because no one should have to put up with that poison from a person they call a friend. Friends care about how you feel.'

A frown creased her forehead at the thought of him kissing her again. That could *so* not happen.

'Thirdly. No matter what you may think of me, the simple fact is we've proved we can work together these last few days. Not everyone could put up with what you dish out. If you think you can work better with someone else, then you should go right ahead and change—' he stepped closer '—but it's like this. You need to trust someone to help you get where you want to be. And I get the impression that's not something you're very good at. So keep in mind that in a couple of months you won't ever have to set eyes on me again. So no matter what you say to me, or what information you trust me with to help you get where you want to be, it won't matter. You'll never see me again, even if you still keep coming to the gym. I won't be here. I'll be going away again soon.'

Cara stared.

'You said that everything that woman said was based on the truth?'

She nodded.

'Including the bit about hiding away since you broke up with your ex?'

That bit was true. Kind of. But it wasn't entirely because of Niall. When she had a deadline looming, she often disappeared from the outside world for weeks at a time. It came with the territory. But she was curious as to where Rory was going with all this. And every time she opened her mouth around him she seemed to drop herself in it.

So she stayed silent, pursing her lips tightly together to stop any more information from slipping out.

And nodded again.

'Did he by any chance do the usual and throw personal stuff at you to hurt you before you broke up?'

Oh, he had *no idea*.

She swallowed. 'Everyone does that.'

'So he did, then?'

Cara swallowed harder. He was on the right track, too close to things she hadn't discussed with anyone. But a smaller answer would escape the great analysis. 'Yes.'

Another step closer. And this time his large body was so close to hers that they were almost touching. Never in her life had Cara felt so small, so overwhelmed by the presence of a man. It was a highly sensitizing thing as it happened. While her heart thundered in her chest as she waited for him to make his point, she was also deeply aware of how the air seemed to heat up several degrees between their bodies, of how his now familiar scent was surrounding her, of how she was focused on the sound of his breathing and evening hers out to match it.

She practically went weak at the knees.

'Well, there's no danger of that happening if you trust me, Cara. You're not just here to tone up for some stupid bridesmaid's dress. You're trying to make some changes. I get that. It's what most people who come here do, I'd guess. So use me.' He shrugged, a smile forming in his eyes and at the corners of his mouth at the two tiny words laced with suggestion. 'Use and abuse all you want and get whatever it is that's bugging you out of your system. Then I'll have done a good job. And I could do with achieving something positive about now.'

The smile he gave her was infectious. And even though she knew he'd probably used that smile hundreds of times to get women to come around to his way of thinking, she couldn't help but be sucked in by it. He really was something.

Her mouth was suddenly quite dry.

Maybe by 'using him' as he was inviting her so she *could* work her way through some stuff. He was an outsider from her little world, a stranger with no preconceptions of the kind of person she was. And she'd never see him again. It was a golden opportunity. Of sorts. If she were brave enough to accept it.

Which, realistically, she would never have been before. But this was the great transformation of Cara, wasn't it?

Thing was, she wasn't the kind of person who could try out an offer like that without reciprocation of some kind. What he would expect in return was equally terrifying to her. Was job satisfaction really enough reward? If it was, then he wasn't charging enough for his services.

And what would he require if he expected more? Would it involve any degree of nakedness?

Cara tried really hard to focus her mind away from the idea of him naked. He'd be simply glorious, wouldn't he?

All right, so he could have no idea that walking down that aisle behind her friend as a renewed Cara would be one of the best moments of her life. One she was sorely in need of. So he had no way of knowing how great a temptation it was to her to accept him.

Temptation. She swallowed. She was thinking naked Rory again. *Stop it, Cara! Back to the offer on the table.*

Even though she really didn't know him that well, and would never see him again, to have a gift like that handed to her on a platter couldn't go unrewarded without having some of the shine taken off it.

Which brought her back to what he might expect in return. And the whole nakedness thing. Tempting as that vision was, it couldn't happen. This wasn't a man who would understand someone not responding to his *ministrations.*

No matter how much she would love to. Low down inside. Low, *low* and *deep* down inside.

She swallowed a moan at the thought, her addled brain looking for something else she could do in return. Finally picking up on the last thing he'd said.

'Why do *you* need something positive about now?'

The smile faded and shadows darkened his eyes again, 'That doesn't matter.'

Oh, nice try. 'I think it does. Trust is a two way thing, you know.'

Rory took some time to think that one over. The shadows remained in his eyes as he looked away from her face, this time to a point over her head. Then he looked back down as a decision was made, a shrug of his shoulders almost intimating the throwing of something heavy off them.

'I let some people down a few months ago.'

'Did you mean to let them down?'

'I could have tried more not to, I think. It was my job to try.'

'And you can't forgive yourself?'

'Not so much.'

Cara tilted her chin as she thought, looking at him from the corner of her eye in a way that could easily have been interpreted by a bystander as flirtation. 'I'm not the only one who needs to work through some stuff, then.'

The corners of his mouth twitched briefly. 'Maybe not.'

'W-e-l-l—' she smiled the most open smile she had at him since they'd met, her eyes sparkling '—as the archetypal caveman type that's probably not an easy thing for you to work your way through.'

Rory looked as if he was finding it tough to keep his smile at bay. 'Could be.'

And Cara found herself suddenly enjoying talking to him. It felt better to be on more even ground, as if she actually had a little more control. Lord only knew it had been a while since she'd felt that way. And boy, oh, boy did it feel *good*.

'It's like this, you see. For us to work together there has to be some trust. And I get the impression it's been a while since you trusted someone.'

The smile escaped and lit up his eyes as she used his own reasoning against him. 'So, you think maybe 'cos I'll never see you again after a couple of months that maybe I'll find some security in that?'

Cara nodded sagely. 'I do.'

A deep grumble of laughter tumbled up from his chest. 'You're something, you know that, right?'

'You bring out the worst in me.'

'Actually, I don't agree with that.'

'No surprise there, then.'

The laughter faded, but the diamond bright sparks remained in his dark eyes as he made a drama out of sighing before he leaned his face closer to hers and asked, 'So?'

'So.' She did her best not to be disconcerted by how close his mouth was to hers, of how in another life and in another body it would have taken very little effort to reach forwards and claim that mouth. To see if her last physical reaction had been a one-off brought on by the element of surprise. If it wasn't, then maybe even to get lost for a while and solve some problems with the simple satisfaction brought by basic lust.

But she was a long way off being confident enough to make that kind of a move, wasn't she?

With that regret in her mind she refused to allow herself another one to keep it company. The new Cara could take a chance. She could!

'So, I guess I can try if you can.'

He studied her face, searching one eye and then the other, before his gaze ran slowly over the rest of her face, lingering on her mouth for a moment longer than it had anywhere else. Then he nodded. 'Then I guess I'll see you same time tomorrow and we'll start over. As friends.'

CHAPTER FIVE

'I'D RATHER CRAWL over hot coals.'

Rory laughed aloud at her deadpan expression. 'It's not that big a deal. It'll be a good way of relaxing your muscles from this. *And* you'll still be working out.'

'I'm not doing it.'

'I thought you'd agreed to try and trust me.'

'I did. But it didn't involve getting pretty much naked in a public place.'

'You won't be naked. I can lend you one of the club's suits. They're very tame. And there won't be anybody else there; the place closes in twenty minutes.'

'Well, then, we don't have time.'

'You have me to train with; I can stay here as long as I like after hours. And I need to do a few laps for my leg.' He bent over, grasped her hands in his and tugged her upright. 'C'mon.'

Upright, her body almost touching all along the hard length of his, she scowled up at him. But it wasn't a scowl because she was mad at him. In fact, the workout so far had been much more fun than she would have thought working out could ever have been. As if their truce and temporary 'friendship' had helped make things more relaxed.

No, this scowl had much more to do with the whole, 'being partially naked in *his* company' issue. One step at a time to the rebuilding of her confidence and all that…

And she'd already seen some of the club's swimwear. Rory might have thought it tame, but it wasn't exactly top-to-toe covering. In fact, just paint it red and you had the kind of costumes busty blondes wore on Californian lifeguard TV shows.

'Would it make you feel any better if I let you go do your laps alone and waited 'til you were gone to do mine?'

Hell yes.

But this was all about creating a new Cara, wasn't it? And they'd already agreed what the other thought wouldn't matter in a few months. She could do this. She could pretend that it didn't matter to her whether Rory looked at her and liked what he saw.

She could.

Even if she cajoled herself by telling her fluttering stomach it would be better if he didn't like what he saw. If he did, he might feel the need to do something about it.

So, she pinned a smile in place. 'No, that's dumb. You'll be wanting to get home, too, so it makes sense to swim together. And, anyway, I need you there to make sure I don't drown.'

Which was a bit of a fib actually.

'Exactly. You stay under longer than ten minutes and I'll call for help.' He winked. 'I'll throw a suit in through the door of the changing rooms and check that Sam can lock the front doors. So I'll meet you in the water.'

Great. That meant if she rushed she could be in the water before he got there. That would help. Then all she would have to do was work out how to get back out again with some dignity. Maybe if she suggested he tried staying under for ten minutes and she called to see if anyone *actually* turned up?

As it was, she was in the pool for more than those ten minutes before he reappeared. And it was a little corner of mind numbing heaven. She'd forgotten how much she loved to swim.

In the dim light of the deserted pool it was bliss. The warm water lapped around her body as she floated off the side, her head resting against the raised tiles while she looked at the light reflecting off the ceiling.

Rory had been right. It was helping her to forget the aches in her muscles. It also gave her thinking time. Which inevitably brought her to *thinking* about Rory, which she'd been doing a lot of since their 'truce', truth be told.

No matter how much she tried not to.

In fact, lazing about in the water, her body relaxed and soothed, she was very conscious of the fact that she was waiting for him. Not doing the laps she was supposed to be doing. Just waiting.

As if swimming was the last thing on her mind.

There had never been anyone who had had such a profound effect on her deepest, darkest thoughts as he did. All right, so maybe darkest wasn't exactly the right word. Dirtiest would be closer. He was just so all-fired sexual. Everything about him calling out to her on the most basic of levels.

Cara had always known there was that side to her. But she had never met someone who so vividly illustrated it to her. If he had a single notion of the contents of her dreams of late! She'd been waking up with tangled sheets, her body soaked with perspiration, and just plain wet.

Maybe she should try her hand at writing some erotica? Under a different name of course. No point in alienating all those nice people who already bought what she wrote…

A door opened at the other end of the pool and Cara's eyes shifted to watch as he walked in. Her eyelids heavy with the thoughts she'd been having.

Oh, boy. Well, *he* obviously wasn't bothered with walking around practically naked in public. And she'd been right. He was, indeed, glorious.

If he spent more time walking around looking like that she'd bet her house the female membership at the gym would triple in a day. There wasn't a hint of self-consciousness about him as he walked to the deep end where she was and Cara really wanted to hate him for that. But then he had nothing to be self-conscious about, did he? Was it any wonder he was so arrogant?

Despite the fact she knew his dark eyes were fixed on her,

Cara decided to make an intensive study of him while he was on display, just to be sure of her facts. Research for all that erotica…

There wasn't an ounce of superfluous fat on him. But then, as the owner of a gym, it wouldn't look good if there was, would it? But he wasn't some pumped-up steroid user—oh, no. He had the look of someone who had that body without even trying. Who was as comfortable with his inner strength as his outer.

From the broad width of his shoulders, across the expanse of muscled chest, peppered with dark hair that veed down towards his navel and disappeared into the waistband of his shorts. From the flat washboard waist, past the thankfully loose fit of his shorts, to the long length of his legs. Every inch of him was all male.

And in a room full of water, her mouth went dry.

The only thing out of place was his slight limp.

While Cara swallowed hard, he turned the corner of the pool and she frowned as she sought the source of his limp. Her brain having already been distracted by the fact that he was deeply tanned, all over—a rarity for an Irish native—she had failed to notice the scarring. But from her position as he turned she saw a distinct change in colour on one thigh. There the skin was pinker, creased. And in the centre of the scarring was a distinct dimpled circle.

Her eyes rose to his in question as he looked down at her.

And he smiled wryly in return. 'Yeah, I know, ruins my attempt at being a perfect specimen of manhood.'

Not so much, as it happened. 'What did you do?'

'I didn't do anything, barring get in the way.'

'Of what?'

She saw him hesitate, saw how he looked down at the water as he bent over and swung his arms back and forth in preparation for a dive, the muscles in his shoulders flexing. Then he glanced at her from beneath the wisps of dark hair that had fallen over his forehead and shrugged, 'Of the bullets from some guy's gun.'

While Cara gaped in surprise, he dived neatly into the water, throwing droplets into her face that she had to blink away before she launched herself off the side of the pool. He waited at the other end until she caught him, then adjusted his speed so that they were swimming side by side.

'So what really happened?'

He smiled as he swam, turning onto his back. 'I just told you what happened.'

'You're telling me someone shot you?' She turned her head and studied him as she did the breast stroke, pulling herself through the water with surprising ease, considering how long it had been since she'd last been in the water. 'With an actual gun?'

'No, with a cannon. It just had teeny little balls for ammunition.' He chuckled at his own joke.

'You gotta watch out for that in downtown Dublin, right enough. I tell you, the number of times a tank has taken my parking spot at the shopping centre.' She tutted and looked down the pool, concentrating on her swimming. 'But if you didn't want to talk about it you only had to say so.'

'I am talking about it. You're just choosing not to believe me.'

Cara scowled as he turned over again, executed an underwater turn and powered ahead of her. Forcing her to push harder to catch up with him. 'Well, how am I supposed to believe something like that? Next you'll be telling me you're some kind of secret agent. It's just good to know the trust thing is going so well for us.'

He broke stroke to tread water. And with that she pushed harder again and made it to the deep end of the pool before him. But he wasn't far behind.

The next thing she knew, there was a large hand around her ankle and he tugged hard, just the once, which put her head momentarily underwater.

Spluttering, she came up for air and struggled free, turning her back against the pool edge. Treading water, she pushed her hair back off her face, blinking the water out of her eyes in time to see him get up close and personal.

Uh-oh.

His large hands landed on either side of her waist while he

moved his body in against hers to pin her in place. 'I'm not lying, Cara. I did get shot. Six months ago in the Middle East. I did tell you I'm not here much. A couple of dozen times now, if I recall.'

Trying really, really hard to ignore the fact that the sliding water was brushing her body closer to his, she swallowed and tried to focus on the sincerity in his dark eyes. She'd believe he was the Easter Bunny at this stage if he would just move a little farther away from her.

The other end of the pool would do.

She didn't need the hard length of him so close to her, didn't need his hands holding her in place, didn't need her pulse beating harder in her veins or her mouth going dry again. She'd known getting into the pool was a bad idea! Why, oh, why did she let herself get talked into these things?

'Fine, I believe you.' She squirmed back tighter against the wall, arms reaching out on either side for a firm grip on the edge of the tiles, while her heart beat harder against her breastbone.

Rory laughed a low laugh. 'No, you don't.'

'Sure I do. You can let go now.'

'Not 'til I think you really believe me.'

'If you say you were shot then you were shot. Fine. Gotcha.' She attempted a convincing smile and squirmed again. 'Let go and we'll do some more laps.'

'I'm serious.' The intensity in his dark eyes told her that her attempt at being convincing hadn't actually gone all that well. 'I'm only home a few months each year. I work for a company that supplies escorts for oil workers and construction crews in problem areas. And we got ambushed. And I got shot.'

'Okay.' She squirmed a little harder, looking around the pool for a means of escape.

'I'm not letting you go 'til you look me right in the eye and say you believe me.'

If all else failed she'd try that, even if it was tough to accept what he was saying. 'I believe you.'

When she forced herself to look him in the eye, her breath

hitched. Oh, boy. He really was hot. On fire, in fact. And he was within kissing distance again. And they were in a swimming pool, alone.

The possibilities grew exponentially in her mind.

'What's wrong?'

'Nothing's wrong. I already told you, I believe you. You're some kind of Rambo-type bodyguard. Good for you.'

There was silence as the water, shifted by her constant squirming, splashed up and over the tiles behind her head. Then Rory's hands tightened a fraction against her waist, his eyes glittering. 'Do you get this bothered every time someone touches you? Or is it just that it's me touching you?'

Cara scowled at his half a misinterpretation, not that she was about to tell him what was really going on!

'Don't be ridiculous. I just don't like being bullied into place.'

Ignoring the glare she gave him he moved closer, so that his body slid along the length of hers, slick with the warm water between them.

'That's not all of it though, is it?'

'What the hell else would it be? You're just ticked off because I'm not throwing myself at you like other women probably do!'

She struggled even harder as the truth almost spilled out. Even while half of her warred with the other half. Keep fighting him off and risk him taking it as an invitation. Or stay still. And risk him taking it as an invitation.

It was a devil-and-the-deep-blue-sea situation.

Cara couldn't risk him accepting any kind of an invitation, subliminal or otherwise. As active as her imagination was, she wouldn't be able to follow it through. Not to the kind of conclusion a man like him would expect, anyway. And she'd rather stay frustrated and unrequited than, well, frustrated and mortified. Which was bound to happen.

'Do you think I'd hurt you?' His face darkened at the suggestion, while his mind came up with an alternative solution to her reaction to his proximity. 'What the hell kind of guys were you involved with before?'

Cara stilled, her chin rising an inch, 'Don't be daft! Do I really look that desperate?'

Please don't say she looked that desperate!

'I'd like to hope not, too.' The hold on her waist softened a little, and his thumbs brushed back and forth against her stomach. 'So what's wrong?'

She pursed her lips.

Which teased a smile back onto the corners of his mouth. 'Go on, you can do it. You can talk to me.'

'Not about this one, I can't.'

'Why not?'

'Because it's *personal*. As in private, don't want-to-discuss-it personal.'

'Not because you don't trust yourself to share stuff with me?'

'You really are very pushy.'

'I've been told that.'

She made another attempt to push back from him, any small distance at all that would take her breasts away from being pressed against the hard wall of his chest. Because she really wasn't coping well with how that made her feel; the now-familiar flames that licked up inside her, the brand-new addition of goose bumps on her flesh.

The fact that she was using her arms stretched out on the pool edge behind her to stop from sinking meant she couldn't use her hands to push him away. Which was maybe just as well. Touching his naked chest in the water would make their position even more intimate than it already was.

It would make it all that much easier to smooth those hands over his slick skin, to work around the column of his neck where her fingers could tangle in his wet hair. Which was tempting, there was no arguing that...

And something that every nerve end in her body seemed to be baying for. It was almost too cruel for words. Because what her body craved, her mind couldn't see through to a logical conclusion. No matter how much she might have wanted it to, just once. Even the *one time*.

She sighed, a deeply heartfelt sigh. 'You're not going to quit on this, are you?'

He shook his head very, very slowly.

So Cara swore beneath her breath.

Then his legs brushed against hers under the water as he used them to stay afloat, coarse hair grazing against smooth skin, his muscled thigh brushing against the rounded curves of hers. And while he continued looking at her with those intense eyes of his, she couldn't think much about anything.

Except sex.

Which was exactly where the conversation was headed; little did he know it.

His deep voice took on a persuasive tone, 'Trust, remember?'

'All right, fine.' Her irritation at the predicament he'd put her in came through in her tone. 'You want the whole big deep analysis of the thing, then I'll break it down into simple terms for you so we can get it over and done with. Then this never need come up again.'

She frowned hard at her choice of words as his legs brushed hers again. 'Look, I'm sure that you're a very sexually charged man and all that. You're bound to be, looking the way you do and all. And it's a guy thing after all, strongest of the species, et cetera, et cetera, et cetera…'

Rory smiled at her words. 'That's right, distract me with flattery. That'll work every time.' He looked at the ceiling, took a breath and looked back at her. 'With anyone but me. *I'm* not so easily distracted from the things I want.'

'Well, I'm just making an observation.' She gulped, ignored the 'I want' part and tilted her head. 'Are you going to deny it?'

He used the hands on her waist to pull her a little away from the wall, and wrapped one of his ankles around one of hers to hold her in place. Then he dropped his voice to a husky tone.

'That right now, you would appear to be the kind of thing I might want? No, right now this second, I'm not going to deny that. You can't tell me being here in the water like this isn't doing something for you, too. Where's your sense of adventure?'

Actually, she'd meant the strongest of the species part. And now she really couldn't breathe.

With the water surrounding them, she could feel the friction between their bodies in a purely sensual way, her curves fitting in against the hard dips and planes of him. And they fitted everywhere, from ankle to shoulder, her breasts rubbing against the hair on his chest with only the fine layer of her wet costume holding skin from skin. She'd quite honestly never been so turned on in her entire life, which made a complete lie out of what she said next,

'The thing is, I'm not.'

'Not what?' His face came closer to hers. 'Not as turned on by us being this close as I am?'

She couldn't be that blatantly dishonest, but neither could she say that big a thing out loud. 'Not very highly sexually charged. I'm really not. So there's not much point in you touching me or flirting with me, because it's not going to lead to anything.'

'You think you're not highly sexually charged?'

'I know I'm not. I didn't get to this age without knowing myself.'

Moving his hands round to her back, he encircled her waist with his arms and held her closer still. Then he hitched her up and back down, moving the water between them and increasing the friction of her breasts against the hard wall of his chest.

When she gasped, he smiled. A slow, sensual smile. 'I disagree. I think there's plenty of sexual charge here. And it's not just from me.'

Cara felt a lump form in her throat. This kind of thing was probably a daily occurrence for someone like him, and probably for the kind of women he normally spent time with. In and out of swimming pools. But not for her. She'd always been the chubby girl at school, when all the other girls had been off exploring their new-found sexuality with their chosen boyfriends. And the chubby girl with the sarcastic mouth hadn't been the one the boys had wanted to explore with. So she'd been a late bloomer.

A late bloomer whose first real sexual experiences had been far removed from the descriptions in magazine articles and romance novels, which had left her feeling inadequate and self-conscious right up into her early twenties.

And then she'd ended up with Niall.

Oh, her body was fully aware of everywhere it was touching Rory's, there was no arguing that. Any more than she could argue the heavy pool of heat that had settled between her legs. But it still couldn't lead to anything. And it wasn't fair to let Rory believe it could.

'Okay.' Her voice was still a little breathless so she cleared her throat. 'I'm not going to argue that part—'

'Write down the time and date, quick.' He grinned across at her, his dark eyes sparkling in triumph. 'We finally agree on something. It's about damn time.'

He leaned in closer, angling his head as he looked up into her eyes with a sparkle of amusement in his.

But Cara leaned her head back out of his way.

'Don't do that. Really, there's no point in flirting with me. Nothing's gonna happen. *I mean it.*'

Thick dark lashes flickered upwards as his brows rose in question. 'Who said something had to happen? But at least I'm learning something about you. Not the casual sex type, I take it?'

'Not the sex type in general.'

Her words widened his eyes in disbelief. 'You're celibate?'

'Not celibate. Well, yes, kind of. It's not that I haven't. I mean, obviously I have. No one in this day and age gets to twenty-seven without, well, you know. It's just that I don't—'

Her babbling made him smile again. 'Sleep around.'

'Yes. Well, no.' She shook her head and closed her eyes in frustration at her lack of eloquence. 'I don't sleep around. But it's not just that. It's just I can't, well, I don't—'

Oh, this was *ridiculous!* She was making a complete and utter idiot of herself! Which was precisely what she'd been trying to avoid.

'*Cara.*'

She opened her eyes at the firm demand of his deep voice. It took a few moments of blinking before he came into focus so close to her and it was disconcerting as all hell when he did. His steady gaze was enough on its own to make her breath hitch again.

And all the while the water was moving around them and he was constantly adjusting their bodies to keep them both afloat.

The combination made it *very* hard to think rationally.

When she didn't speak he softened his voice. 'Take a few breaths and then tell me what it is you're trying to say. I can take it. I'm a big boy.'

With his lower body touching and parting and touching and parting against her abdomen, she was in *absolutely* no doubt about that.

Oh, boy.

So, she swallowed hard and took a couple of breaths before diving in with the truth. 'It's not that I'm not affected by this. There's no point in lying about that. It's just that there's no point in it and I'm not the kind of girl who leads someone on. There would be certain *expectations,* you see, if we start this whole flirting thing for real instead of it being a game we play.'

'I don't have any expectations. Flirting is flirting. It's a bit of fun is all. It doesn't mean it's written in stone that anything else will happen.'

'Oh, no.' She laughed nervously. 'You might say that now, but enough flirting goes on and you *will* have expectations. You're a man. And if we start this kind of stuff then you know where it will lead in the end. You can't tell me you don't.'

'Fooling around a little if we both feel like doing it isn't anything more than that.'

'But it would be. If we fooled around enough.'

His gaze darkened, but remained steady. 'Not any further than doing something we may well both want to do.'

'And there's an expectation already. See what I mean?'

Rory took a deep breath that expanded his broad chest even further and teased her breasts again. 'And that would be such a very bad thing, would it?'

'*Yes,* it *would.*' She pleaded with him with her eyes, wanting him to understand without her actually having to go through the embarrassment of spelling it out loud. 'Because it wouldn't be all that good.'

There was a tense pause while he stared at her. Then he smiled a purely sexual smile. 'Hon, you'd have to believe that if we ever got that far, I'm more than capable of making it way past good. I take a lot of pride in that fact. Trust me.'

Cara rolled her eyes at his arrogance and moaned a small, agonized moan low in her throat at the effect it had on her. Her body really was making such a liar out of her.

'You see, that's just it. You'd be all male pride about it, determined to make it the most mind-blowing experience of my life or something. Determined that you'd be the best I ever had.'

'And you think I wouldn't be?'

'Damn it, Rory, you're not listening to me!'

'I'm listening to every word. You're just not making any sense.'

'I'm *trying* to be straight with you!' She made another attempt to struggle out of his hold.

But it was as if she were held by bands of steel. And all the struggling was doing was rubbing her body even more against his.

Rory frowned across at her. 'No, you're talking round in circles rather than just coming out with it. I thought we'd already agreed to try a little trust, so you could work through whatever it was you wanted to.'

Cara struggled harder against him, despite her best intentions. 'Would you let go of me, you great oaf? I'm done with this conversation. Let's just leave it at the simple fact that nothing is going to happen so you can just damn well forget it! There are certain things I have no intention of *working my way through* with you. End of story.'

'Fine.' And just like that he let go of her and held his hands up, palms towards her as he kicked back in the water and put some distance between them. 'Calm down. I've never forced myself on anyone. Never had to. But just so you know, whatever the problem is here, we could have talked about it like adults and got past it. Because we have this cut-off point already in place, don't we?'

Cara glared at him, her frustration spilling over the edge. She really had just made a complete babbling idiot of herself, hadn't she? She could have left it alone, joked her way out of it, had a kids' water fight for crying out loud! Something easy and simple and repercussion free. But oh, no, she had to go and dig herself *a hole*.

'Oh, yes, damn it.' She raised one hand from the tiles and clicked her fingers silently. 'I clean forgot. You have this window of opportunity to shag someone and you thought it might help my self-esteem if you chose me! Well, silly me.'

He twisted his body and kicked back towards her, his words spoken with a warning tone. 'Oh, no, you don't. Whatever issues you have with sex have got nothing to do with me. All I've done is flirt with you some. And have the guts to admit I was turned on by where we were. You're the one bringing up the subject of sex, not me. And you've obviously thought this a lot further ahead than I had. So you're either mad with yourself for thinking about it, or angry that I now know you did. You tell me which one it is. But don't make it my fault.'

And he was right. When he stopped a little away, treading water as he glared angrily at her, she felt the back of her throat begin to burn. But she couldn't weaken in front of him. Couldn't let him see that he'd just hit the proverbial nail on the head.

Because the issues she had with sex were nothing to do with him. They were all hers.

'You're right. It's not your fault. But if I let something happen between us, even knowing there was a no-strings-attached clause, my issues would become your issues. And it's not your fault that I don't like sex. But you'd think it was. You're exactly the kind of man who would think it was. And then you'd spend all your time trying to prove yourself until everything went pear shaped and we did nothing but argue.'

Putting her previous embarrassment about being seen by him in a swimsuit to the back of her mind, she turned and hauled herself out of the water, throwing words over her shoulder. 'I'm not looking for you to understand or to help me work out why I can't get the same kick out of the act as other people do. I'm just laying it on the line and being honest with you. Because we both know what just happened here was a *first step.*' She kept walking towards the changing rooms.

'You're the one who wanted me to trust you enough to talk to you, remember? To be completely honest? So there you go. Like the saying goes: be careful what you wish for.'

There was the sound of movement in the water behind her. 'Are you done? Or is there more you need to get off your chest?'

She paused with her hand on the door and swung round to glare at him. 'What else do you need?'

He was out of the water and headed her way. 'Well, you could take a breath and try calming down. The words mountain and molehill come to mind.'

Cara's eyes widened.

But he was on a roll. 'For what it's worth, if something *had* happened beyond flirting, the only expectations I would have had would have been of myself. If I'd had any expectations of you it would have been that you'd have had one hell of a time, because I'd have made quite sure of that.'

'Oh, you really are the most arrogant son of a—'

'It's not arrogance, Cara.' He stopped a few steps from her. 'It's called self-confidence.'

And was something she was obviously sorely lacking in. He didn't have to spell it out for her.

Hand on hip, she smiled her sweetest smile. 'And I think

we're done here, don't you? I don't want you as my trainer any more. Consider yourself fired.'

Rory's eyes darkened dangerously as he frowned at her. 'Fine.'

'*Fine.*'

He shook his head. 'Great.'

'Yes, *isn't it?*'

And with that they both turned and the changing-room doors slammed in unison.

CHAPTER SIX

IT WAS AN ironic fact of life that you could go a lifetime without meeting someone and then, when you didn't want to see them any more, they were right under your nose.

Cara found herself mulling that one over when she saw Rory a week later in a street café in the city centre. With another woman. Nope, strike that. A woman. Saying *another woman* suggested that Cara was *the main* woman, which she wasn't. And neither did she want to be.

This *particular woman,* however, looked nearly as upset as Cara had felt when she'd fled the pool that last day. It was nice to know she wasn't the only woman he had that effect on. It made her feel less useless.

Cara had sat down at her table inside before she saw them, and now she was stuck. She couldn't chance a big retreat in case they saw her this time. So, she did the mature thing, sliding a little lower in her seat, and holding the book she'd bought up in front of her face. Telling herself she was only peeking over it occasionally in case he had spotted her, but admitting after a while that it was more likely in case she missed anything.

Which made her feel incredibly childish.

So she closed the book, setting it down so hard on the table top that her cup rattled on its saucer. Glancing up in momentary panic at the attention-seeking noise, she scowled when she knew she still hadn't been caught. He really did bring out the worst in her, damn him.

The woman looked a little more distressed and Cara felt unwanted jealousy cramp through her midriff as Rory leaned closer and reached an arm around her slender shoulders. Whatever the conversation was, it was troublesome for both of them. Because despite the way he had moved closer to offer comfort, Cara could see the tension in his body, as if he wasn't completely at ease with the closeness.

Yep. It looked like a breakup to her. And one he had instigated. Another one bit the dust….

After a while Rory looked around, which made Cara slide down in her seat again and glance away. Just in case. Spying was one thing. Being caught spying was another. But when she glanced back he was already leaning back, while his companion dabbed at the corners of her eyes with a tissue.

Oh, he really was a piece of work, wasn't he?

Then, while Cara watched from over the rim of her cup, the woman gathered together her bag, squeezed his hand where it lay on the table, and placed a kiss on his cheek before she left.

Cara continued watching as Rory smiled at her, nodded in answer to something she said, raised a hand to wave. Then, when the woman was out of his line of vision, he sighed, and slumped down in his chair, his hands dangling between his legs as he watched the world go by with a dark scowl on his face. He looked heavenwards, leaned forward and looked at his feet. And the scowl stayed in place the whole time.

Whatever had happened had obviously affected him more than he'd let on in front of his partner. Which surprised Cara. If he'd had someone he cared about that much why had he split up with her? And, more to the point, why had he been *flirting* with Cara only a few days before?

She found herself suddenly disappointed in him. Hadn't he said he fought for the things he wanted?

Hell, what was she thinking? She shouldn't give a damn what

he did and didn't do, not after their last confrontation. It took two to make an argument, she had told herself, even if she had started it with her stupid babbling mouth. And a good dose of insecurity.

With a shake of his head, he stood up and checked the total on the receipt left on his table before digging in his pocket for change. Then he glanced round again from under his fringe.

And caught sight of her.

Cara froze. She didn't try to hide, didn't smile in invitation; nothing. She just looked right on back at him, while her heart thundered.

She was caught. Damn it.

Rory's chin rose. He glanced around the half-full café, looked for a moment as if he might just ignore her and walk away. Then looked back her way again.

And made his way to her table.

Towering over her, he buried his large hands in his jean pockets. 'Hi.'

'Hi.' Cara looked up at him, her hands playing with the corner of the book on the table top while she fought to control her breathing. Had the café been so warm when she came in?

'Been here long?'

'Long enough to see the tail end of your breakup.' She felt marginally guilty for the admission. Rory might have been many things, stupid however, was not one of them. 'I take it that's what you meant.'

Dark brows quirked in answer. 'You thought that's what it was, did you?'

'Wasn't it?' Cara feigned nonchalance. 'Not that it's really any of my business, but that was what it looked like from here.'

'Well, as it happens, just for a change, you're wrong.' He pulled his hands out of his pockets, drew out the chair facing her, and sat down. Then leaned back and assumed the familiar pose of folded arms across his chest, his eyes blinking slowly as he stared her down with narrowed eyes. As if he was weighing up whether or not he would deign to talk to her. 'She's the wife of one of the guys who was with me when I got hurt.'

Cara's eyes widened. 'Did he—?'

'Get hurt, too?' He barely waited for her nod. 'Yes.'

'He didn't—?'

'Die? No. He didn't die. But he's still in hospital in the UK.' His jaw clenched as he glanced around the café again, thick brows folding down over his dark eyes as he seemed to be deciding again whether or not to continue. 'He's not doing so good, though. Liz wants me to go see him. That's why she came to see me.'

'She *flew* over to ask you? Couldn't she have rung?'

His mouth quirked with self-deprecation. 'She already tried that.'

Cara hesitated, her eyes widening even more. 'And you turned her down?'

'I didn't say I wouldn't go.'

'But you didn't get on a plane, either.'

'No.' He glanced briefly at her, then towards the doorway, as if he was considering leaving. 'And that was wrong of me. I'll go; first thing tomorrow, probably.'

She studied his profile for a long while, took in the tension she could still see there, the clenching muscle in his jaw, the fold of his brows, the defensive position of crossed arms over his chest. And she could read all those signs. Because she knew how it felt to struggle with something difficult.

She just would never have believed that someone like Rory could get that tangled up, too. It garnered an immediate sense of empathy that she would never have expected to feel for someone like him.

So she leaned forwards on the table, pushing her cup to one side as she lowered her voice, encouraging him to keep talking. 'You don't want to see him though, or you would have gone already. How come?'

He shrugged. 'I wasn't all that mobile for a while.'

'Well, we both know you're plenty mobile now.'

Whoops. That popping noise she could hear would be the can of worms she'd just opened, wouldn't it?

He turned his face back towards her. Pursed his mouth for a moment, then unfolded his arms and leaned over the table in a mirror of her stance, his long fingers barely centimeters from hers on the table top. 'How's the working out going with Sam?'

Cara forced herself to smile. 'Swift change of subject there.'

'Just curious.'

Meaning if it were going badly he'd want to try again? It was tempting. Not that Sam wasn't a great trainer, too, but he just didn't push her the way Rory did. Maybe simply because she wasn't so filled with resentment about how she felt when he was around compared to when Rory was around. The kind of resentment that she had put to good use by focusing it on what she was doing.

And she did miss the back and forth of their sparring. But it was easier to stay away from him, right? For a few hours after she had left the pool, she had even contemplated not going back. But she had paid her membership, and the new Cara in the making refused to go back and ask for that refund. Even though the old Cara had really wanted to go and wallow in hiding for a while.

'It's going fine.'

'You haven't felt the need to tell *him* about any issues you have, then?'

Warmth crept swiftly onto her cheeks as she leaned back in her chair. 'Apparently not.'

'Figure out why you told me yet?'

She sighed and looked away from him, giving the escape route a longing glance herself. 'Right this minute the only figuring I'm doing is that it doesn't take much to understand it's easier to turn the conversation back on me rather than talk about what's bothering you.' With a moment's pause she found the courage to look back into his dark eyes. 'That's what you're doing, isn't it?'

It took a challenging quirk of her arched brows before he

answered her. 'Actually I have no idea why I felt the need to even tell you as much as I already did.'

'Then you'll know how I felt when I did it.'

When he didn't answer, she sighed and gave in to a sudden need to smooth things over. 'Maybe you just needed someone to talk to after the difficult time you had with your friend's wife. She looked very upset before she left.'

'She has a lot to deal with.'

'If her husband is anywhere near as much of a pain in the backside as you can be, then I can understand that.'

The teasing light in her eyes died with his answer.

'Yeah, and I got to keep my leg. Just imagine how bad I'd have been if I'd lost both of them like Richard did.'

Cara felt as if he'd just stolen all the air from around her. It was almost too horrific to be real. But while words of apology lodged in her throat, she watched him push the chair back and stand up.

'I guess we all have issues of some kind to deal with. But then, that's life, isn't it?'

He was halfway up the main street before she caught up with him. Even though his expression when leaving shouldn't have encouraged her to follow him at all. The fact was, in the space of two sentences he had managed to make her feel that anything she had to deal with was completely insignificant. Which, compared to what his friend was dealing with, it was.

And she had a sudden urgent need to make amends.

She caught hold of his arm. 'Wait.'

Looking down at her with a flicker of surprise in his eyes, he stopped. 'What for?'

'Is that why you wouldn't go see him—because you felt guilty that you weren't hurt as badly as he was?'

'You don't know what you're talking about.'

'Not until you explain it to me, I don't. So make me understand. Maybe talking it through might help.'

'Now you see me as some kind of project?'

Cara scowled at the question, swiftly releasing his arm. 'Right, and you didn't see me as exactly that when you met me, did you?'

'No, as a matter of fact, I thought you were sexy as hell the second you walked through the door.'

'Well, now you know that that's the exact opposite of what I am! Which just goes to prove you don't know me any better than I know you.'

They scowled at each other in silence.

Until Rory sighed in frustration and lifted his large hands to her shoulders to turn her around, pushing her towards the nearest shop window.

'What are you doing?' Cara continued scowling at him, this time in reflection, as she dug her heels in and pushed back against his determined direction.

His eyes met hers in the glass, the wares on sale behind it fading out of focus. 'We're making something crystal-clear. If you open your eyes and see what I see then we'll have one less thing to argue about, won't we? So look at yourself. *Really look*. And tell me what you see.'

Cara struggled against his hold. 'This is stupid.'

'No, what's stupid is that two grown people spend as much time arguing as you and me do. And, I don't know about you, but I'm getting *really* tired of it.'

When she stopped struggling, he stepped closer, so that the length of his body was touching all along her back. His eyes stayed locked with hers as he lifted one hand from her shoulder and snaked his arm forward until his thumb and forefinger had her chin, his mouth close to her ear as he whispered in a husky grumble, '*Look*.'

When she tried to turn her head to look up at him, his thumb and forefinger held her in place. Until finally she dragged her eyes away, past his eyes in the reflection, and she looked at herself.

It was something she tried not to do too often. Not because she hated how she looked, not completely. She had her good points, and there was always her 'pretty face' to fall back on. It was just that, like most women, she tended to focus on the bad rather than the good.

And that wasn't what he was asking her to do.

'Really look, Cara. Forget about that giant chip of self-consciousness on your shoulder for a minute. Think like a guy for a second if that's what it takes to see what I see.'

His voice was low, persuasive, soothing, seductive. So she stood and looked, *really* looked. While Rory kept his head tucked in against her shoulder and his thumb on her chin.

And with his body as a frame for hers, for the first time in her life she *felt* sexy. The sight of his large body against hers seemed somehow to put her into proportion. She wasn't the giant Amazon woman in a line of stick-thin bridesmaids, whose dresses all looked so much better on them in her eyes than hers did on her.

Yes, she still curved, there was no doubting that. But against his body those curves didn't look huge and ungainly, they looked womanly, sensuous, a compliment to the harder lines of the powerful male body behind her.

Rory moved his hand from her chin, adjusted his body back to make room for his arm to snake behind her and around her waist, before he fitted back against her, spreading his feet wider. And the sight of that strong arm around her brought her a little taller against him. It tucked the material of her soft sweater tighter against her middle, so that the curve from hip to waist to breast was more pronounced.

The other hand came off her shoulder, made a similar journey between their bodies, before spreading his fingers on either side of her waist, touching from the base of her ribcage to the jut of her hip-bone.

It was so powerfully sexual a sight. One that conjured up a different reflection in her mind: of their naked bodies in the same position. And the erotic mental picture almost drew a low moan from her lips.

Eyes darkening, she looked up and met his again as he smiled slowly, his voice still low as he tilted his mouth closer to her ear. 'See?'

For the first time ever Cara was at a complete loss for words. Through no choice of her own.

Which didn't escape him.

He chuckled, his smile growing as he continued holding her gaze. 'Whether you like it or not, you *are* sexy, Cara Sheehan. There isn't a man on the planet who wouldn't look at you and think that. Women are *supposed* to curve. At least this way, we have one thing crystal-clear.' He took a breath, his deep voice dropping to an almost whisper. 'You didn't give me a chance to talk through everything you said at the pool—'

Finally she found her voice again. 'Is that why you won't talk to me now about your problems?'

The smile faded, but his voice stayed low and intimate while shoppers passed them by. 'You can't help with that. It's something I just have to work through on my own before I go back to work again.'

'You need to talk to someone, though, if it's still bothering you so much that you can't go and see your friend.' She turned around in his hold, lifting her chin so she could continue to look up at him, her hands rising to his arms, fingers flexing around his muscles. 'No matter what I say, we seem to end up with you trying to help me in some way. And I appreciate that. I do. But if we're going to be friends again 'til you leave, then I want that to be a two-way street.'

'And we're friends now, are we?'

Cara searched her mind for her definition of friend. But knew without too much thinking they weren't. What they had between them was tentative at best, and yet still there. Still intense. No matter how much she tried telling herself it wasn't. But then, she'd never known someone like Rory Flanaghan before, so how was she supposed to know what was going on?

There were only the bare facts. They had never met before, because he spent so little time in the country, and she spent most of her time in a small, select group of people. And even with the changes she had planned to her own life, that division would remain.

Which meant that whatever 'relationship' they had was temporary. Just as he had pointed out, when he had suggested they take advantage of that to work through some stuff. Which made sense to someone like her.

Because there was no doubting she had trust issues. Thing was, it would appear she wasn't alone in that.

Which made her feel they were on more even ground.

They had an opportunity to have something that could be brief and free from repercussions or false hopes of longevity. A promise of sorts that there wouldn't be any complications.

She eventually managed a smile, her stomach fluttering nervously. 'Why not? Everyone needs a new friend now and then, even if it's just to fill in time 'til life moves them on.'

'Which it will.' He leaned his head a little closer to enforce the point. 'You need to know there's no doubt about that. I'm not the stay-at-home type.'

'Well, then, maybe you can teach me something about that before you go. I've been meaning to get out more.'

'Maybe I can.' There was a heartbeat of a pause. 'Amongst other things. If you'll let me.'

CHAPTER SEVEN

'YOU LOOK DIFFERENT.'

Cara smiled. 'You think?'

'Yeah, apart from the hair and the new clothes, I mean.' Laura leaned in a little closer and studied her face. 'There's just, *something*. What is it?'

'It'll be the new man.'

Cara wanted badly to slap Moira silly. The fact that, in a roundabout way, she was right, didn't help any. Cara just hated the fact that she was close to the truth. And close to telling *her* version of it thanks to several glasses of something bubbly.

Moira smiled as she leaned across the table, 'He's simply divine, too, I'll bet. Tall, dark, handsome, into fitness… Tell all, Cara.'

Oh, Cara knew what she was doing. It was obvious Moira didn't believe that kiss from the other day. Why would she? It wasn't as if there had been a plethora of men who looked like Rory kissing her before.

So, as she smiled with a spark of mischief in her eyes Cara knew Moira was waiting. Waiting for Cara to babble through to the truth as she normally did. And then probably have the humiliation of Moira asking for his telephone number…

Well, not this time.

'Now, Moira, *you* of all people know a girl should *never* kiss and tell…' Cara quirked an eyebrow and waited for her meaning to sink in.

Moira's face changed. She leaned back as a flush touched her cheeks, then swirled the liquid in the bottom of her champagne flute and smiled brightly. 'Anyone for more champers?'

Laura stared at Cara in silence for a long time after Moira left. Then did a slow hand clap as she smiled. 'That's the first time I've ever seen you stop her in her tracks. Even if I am now curious to know what she was going to say. Bravo. It's about time.'

Cara shrugged, 'She had it coming this time.'

'Absolutely. She can't keep going around being such a scandal monger and subtly criticizing everyone else's life when hers is such a mess. One more married man and we all know she'll have the world record.' She leaned a little closer. 'But I think she's always picked on you 'cos she's so jealous of you. And you never bit back, which made it easy for her to keep going. You've been a martyr to put up with it for so long.'

Turning to face the bride-to-be, Cara frowned. 'What do you mean jealous of me? What the hell does she have to be jealous of?'

Laura shrugged. 'Your success, your brains, your wit, your honesty, your girl-next-door natural prettiness, the fact that everyone loves you so much. It's one hell of a combination to someone like Moira who has to bask in the shade of some married man to make up for her own lack of those things. Well, minus the honesty part, obviously. And the girl-next-door prettiness.'

Her friend's interpretation of things stunned Cara. No way. There was no way that someone who looked like Moira, who had men chasing after her like Moira, could possibly be jealous of her. C'mon! The world just didn't work like that, did it?

Laura laughed at her side. 'You see, that's the thing about you. You're so tough on yourself that it never occurs to you someone else might want to be more like you. Give yourself a break, honey. Would you really have been a bridesmaid so many times if your friends didn't love you to pieces? Huh?'

'It's traditional to ask the single friends. And after the third one I had so much experience it made sense for the rest of you guys to ask me. I know a bridesmaid's duties so well now, I could write a book on it….'

'Well, you should if it's anywhere near as funny as the rest of your books!'

'Humour sells, babe.' Cara grinned. 'Second down the best-sellers list from sex, don't you know.'

'And speaking of which—' she leaned in closer '—*is* there a new man on the go?'

'Not in the way you're thinking, no.'

Laura didn't look convinced. 'You sure about that? There's a kind of glow about you. And it'd be about time, you know. You've been out of circulation way too long since Niall left. And we all knew he was wrong for you.'

Hello? Where had that little piece of information been when she'd needed it? And as for the glow? Well. Chalk that one up to a newly discovered sexual awareness and several glasses of champers, right? That, and a new make-up kit to go with the hairdo. It had been years since she'd spent so much money pampering herself.

All part of the great plan.

Laura kept going, this time reaching out to squeeze Cara's hand as she spoke. 'I know you thought he was the one….'

She did? Cara frowned. *Had she?* If she had, it didn't bode well for her in the future, did it?

'But really, I think you were just too good for him and he knew it. You're both better off with other people.' Her face brightened as she looked over Cara's shoulder. 'And if there isn't a new man on the go already, then there's one headed this way that looks like he might be interested. He's been eyeing you up from the bar for ages.'

Cara looked over her shoulder as the tall man made his way through the crowd, smiling at her when she caught his eye. He wasn't half-bad, as it happened. But she had never actually been picked up in a nightclub before. And she wasn't sure she wanted to be now.

That wasn't in the plan. But then neither was a Rory Flanaghan…

She looked back at Laura when her hand was squeezed again.

And was rewarded with a wink. 'Any bit of wonder girl, when you're looking so damn good…'

'See, wall-to-wall women. Just what the doctor ordered!'

Rory's body rocked forward with the force of the 'pat' on his back. So he glared over at his brother. 'Didn't you have enough fun to last a lifetime on your holiday? Sun, sea, sand and women galore, you said. I think you even added a "way-hey" to the end of the sentence…'

'You can never have enough of any of those things. And anyway, we're not here for me, we're here for you. It's about time you got out and socialized again. And you've looked like the end of the world was nigh since you got off the plane this afternoon.'

It had only been a short visit. But it had been enough to do some good, to make amends for the fact he hadn't gone sooner, and to talk about happier memories from before they'd been ambushed.

Okay, so they hadn't talked through the things that were bugging him; things that, even though she meant well, Cara had spotted but couldn't possibly understand.

Even if he had felt a need to tell her, what would have been the point? If he didn't feel someone who had lived it with him would be able to help….

Though, telling her as much as he had was already beyond unusual for him.

Women as work associates. Women as short term girlfriends. *Sure.* Women as people he could share his thoughts with, even the thoughts that troubled him at night? *Uh-uh.*

So maybe his brother Connor had it right. Maybe what he needed was some uncomplicated female company to briefly take his mind off other things.

Like Cara, for instance.

Because she'd been occupying his thoughts almost obsessively of late and that couldn't be a good thing. Not when she kept knocking him back so often and still left him wanting to come back for more.

And he hadn't forgotten that kiss. Or how her eyes had flamed when she'd been held against his body in the pool. Or how she had fought when her body had clearly said it wanted more. Or how she had then, in a roundabout way, issued one hell of a challenge to him.

She was complicated. And way too fascinating for his own good. Blotting her out of his thoughts was the better plan all round, he reckoned.

Especially after an afternoon of being reminded how complicated his life already was.

It was a tad unfortunate, then, that when they turned round at the bar, beers in hand, to survey what was on offer, the first woman Rory set eyes on was Cara.

With another man.

It was like being gut punched.

He turned away. But facing back towards the bar didn't help, thanks to the large mirrors on the back wall. He watched as the man laughed at something she'd just said, his arm over the back of her chair as if it belonged there. Was he the elusive ex that she was so keen to impress?

The scum who had let her think she was somehow lacking in their sexual relationship? Because Rory wasn't so dumb that he hadn't figured that out when she'd left the pool that night.

So why would she want him back?

If she really did want him back, then she wasn't doing too shabby a job of it that Rory could see.

She looked amazing.

He got a better view of her as they stood up, the man reaching for her hand as they headed towards the dance floor. She had done something to her hair, hadn't she? Instead of sitting in a straight line to her shoulders, it was flicking out at the ends, framing her face in a quirky manner that hinted at her personality. And as for her clothes. Well, he'd been right from the start about her curving in all the right places.

She raised her free hand as they started to dance and placed pink fluffy rabbit ears on her head, her face lit up with amusement.

Rory turned round again, his eyes scanning the room. Past his brother and the woman he was already hitting on beside him at the bar, to the sea of heads around them. There were several pairs of fluffy rabbit ears dotted around. What the—?

One owner of fluffy ears turned her back to him and he spotted the sign pinned to her back. A giant 'L' for Learner. Ah-ha…

Cara had said she was due to be a bridesmaid, hadn't she? This was obviously the hen night. And if it was a hen night, then there was no way her ex would be there. Members of the groom's party didn't go to the hen night, not that Rory knew of. Which meant that whoever this guy was, he wasn't the ex. Which meant more than likely he'd come to the nightclub looking for the same thing that Connor had brought Rory to look for.

Well. Rory took a long swallow of beer and made his way towards them through the crowd. It wasn't happening on his watch.

Cara's laughter froze when she saw him. Then her eyes widened. Her partner, however, wasn't too observant, and chose her moment of hesitation to take hold of her waist and swing her round in circles in time to the music.

So Rory spread his legs a little wider apart, folded his arms across his chest in such a way that he still had hold of his beer bottle, and waited. While Cara met his eyes at least once during each spin.

Which made him smile.

As the music changed to something slower she pulled free from her partner and shouted something up at him. He nodded, shouted something back, and then walked away. Which was when Rory would fully have expected her to make her way towards him.

But this was Cara. She never did what he expected her to. She stood in the middle of the mass of moving bodies, tilted her head and raised her eyebrows at him.

Which made him laugh aloud.

The challenge kind of lost its effect when accompanied by pink rabbit ears.

So, after a standoff of a few moments he unfolded his arms, set his beer on the nearest table, and walked over to her. Without a word, he wrapped his arms around her waist, hauled her in tight against him, and began to move them.

'Nice ears.'

'What are you doing here? I thought you were away for a few days.'

'I was. I got back a few hours ago.'

'You weren't gone long.'

'Maybe I missed you.'

She laughed. 'Sure you did.'

Dark eyes moved over her face, taking in the way her eyes looked larger and bluer with her make-up, the way her mouth looked fuller and moister with its deep pink lipstick, the way her skin almost glowed. Then he blinked slowly and asked in a deep voice, 'So who's your friend? I sincerely hope I didn't scare him away.'

Which was what he'd planned on doing.

She laughed again. 'I'm sure he's around somewhere.'

'Planning on coming back, is he?'

Cara tossed her hair back from her cheek and smiled the kind of smile she'd never aimed Rory's way before. 'He might. Depends on whether or not you keep standing over me all bodyguard-like.'

Rory smiled down at her, both amused and turned on by her obvious flirting. 'You wouldn't by any chance be a teeny bit the worse for wear, would you, Cara Sheehan?'

She blinked and pouted. 'Who, me?'

'Your friend plied you with drink, did he?'

'The girls were doing shots earlier. But I only had a couple. And then some champagne. And then Darren bought me a glass of wine. Or two. I forget now.'

The thought of what *Darren* might have expected for those drinks made Rory want to go find him for a quiet word. Instead he held her even closer and guided their movements, trying his absolute best not to be as bad as the recently departed Darren and get turned on by her lush body swaying with his.

It wasn't easy.

Cara then helped loads by wrapping her arms around his neck and pressing her breasts in against his chest before she leaned closer to him to say, 'I'm having the most amazing night, actually.'

Rory chuckled, mentally allowing himself to be included in that accolade. She was pleased to see him. That was progress. 'So I see.'

She smiled at him, blue eyes sparkling. 'I meant before you got here it was amazing. I've had a revelation or two.'

He raised a dark eyebrow. 'From Darren?'

'I haven't known Darren long enough for him to reveal anything.'

And it was damn well staying that way, too. 'So your night was amazing *before* you saw me—how?'

She continued to smile. 'I didn't mean that as an insult.'

'Sure you didn't.'

'We already made peace.'

'Yes, we did.'

'Well, then, shut up and listen.'

He grinned. Then he moved his hands up and down on her back, smoothing his fingertips over the soft material of her light top.

And watched as her eyelids grew heavy in response.

She sighed. 'You like to be in charge even when you're doing what you're bid, don't you?'

'I'd answer that but I was already told to shut up. So tell me about your amazing night.'

'You'd have been proud of me. I stopped Moira mid-flow.'

'That so-called friend from the gym that day?'

'That's the one.' She made an exaggerated nod of her head, rabbit ears bobbing. 'She tried to be smart again and I put her down. First time I've let myself do that.'

'So what changed to make you do it this time?'

The question silenced her, a small vertical frown of concentration appearing between her luminescent eyes as she thought it over. Then she looked up at him, searched from one dark eye to the other while he watched.

He had to lean closer to hear her answer.

'It was just time, I guess.'

He nodded slowly in understanding.

Cara continued to stare up at him while he let his fingertips rove over her back. And she didn't stop him, didn't pull away, she just swayed with him while thoughts crossed over her expressive eyes. Rory realized he'd never met anyone he could see thinking before. *Another Cara-ism.* It gave him a warm feeling of affection towards her at a time when he would usually have seen the opportunity to make a move.

Yep. As he'd thought before: complicated.

'How did it go with your friend?'

Well, that was what he got for not making a move when the opportunity arose. His fingers stilled for a heartbeat and then resumed their gentle exploration. 'Not as bad as I thought it would be and worse than I thought it would be.'

'Can I ask you a question about when it happened?'

'Can I stop you?'

A smile. 'No. But you could choose to avoid answering me like you usually do. Except this time I'm having an amazing night, so you can't turn the conversation back onto me so handy. I'm already making progress, you see.'

'Yes, I do see.' And he preferred this openly confident Cara to the one who had been carrying so much aggression when he'd first met her. Even the way she looked told him she was happier with herself. Did that mean she had forgotten about chasing after her ex, too?

'So, when it happened, were you in charge?'

The question surprised him. 'How did you know that?'

'Female intuition.'

He smiled.

Cara giggled in return. 'It was just a few of the things you said about letting people down and the fact that you're so bossy in everything else you do. You're a take-charge kinda guy, so I assumed that meant you were in a responsible position in your work, too.'

Which meant she'd been thinking about him while he'd been away. That deserved a little honesty in response. 'I'm what they call a Team Leader.'

'So you *were* in charge when you got ambushed.'

'Yes.'

'So, in your mind, does that automatically mean you should have been able to do something to stop it?'

His smile faded as a familiar heaviness came back to his chest. But at the point where he would normally clam up or change the subject, he surprised both of them by answering her honestly again. 'There's no way anyone can predict when or where a team gets hit. And it wasn't the first time we'd run into trouble on that route. It was just the first time any real damage was done.'

'But you still think you could have done something to stop it, don't you?'

This time he didn't answer her.

So she smiled softly. 'That's what I figured.'

Rory shook his head. If they were going to have an intimate conversation, then a nightclub wasn't the place to do it.

'All right, I'm gonna stop quizzing you for now. That's probably as much as you've told anyone in a while anyway.'

'Yes, it is.'

'I know.' She tilted her head and smiled again. 'I'm just glad that I'm not the only one who goes telling someone I barely know things that I've not talked about to anyone else. It evens the playing field out.'

Yes, it did. Which, for someone who was used to being in charge of every relationship he'd ever had with a woman, was a rare thing.

A glance away from her face brought an approaching Darren into his line of vision.

'You almost done here for the night?'

'Yeah, I think this place closes soon.'

'Right, then.' Releasing her, he folded her hand in his and pulled her off the dance floor, away from Darren. 'I'll take you home.'

And he couldn't resist a warning glance over his shoulder as he drew her away. It only took the one.

If anyone was going to spend time with this newly confident version of Cara, it damn well wasn't Darren.

Rory frowned hard at the idea of him or any other man taking advantage of her slightly inebriated state. He'd punch every damn one of them if they tried.

The soft hand enfolded in his squeezed gently, drawing his attention back to her face as she smiled again, a question in her eyes.

And he felt an answering smile form in his chest before it made its way up to his face.

Nope. For the time being she was all *his*.

CHAPTER EIGHT

HE WAS STILL holding her hand.

Of all the things that her night out had given her to think about, that was the one thing that Cara's mind focused on. He had taken her hand to guide her off the crowded dance floor, he had held it while she'd let Laura know she was leaving and through the brief introduction she'd made, he'd held it while she scooped up her handbag and as they'd threaded through the crowd to the exit.

And he was still holding it as they made their way along the leafy streets to her house.

While she smiled happily beside him.

She only lived three streets away. Her entire world in a microcosm, as it happened. Hence why she had chosen a gym so close to home. It was cozy, she had told herself over the years; held a sense of comfort in its familiarity.

There was nothing cozy or safe about having her hand held by Rory, though. Oh, no. Since the first day, when he had encircled her wrist with his hand and stopped her from leaving, she had always had a physical reaction to his touch. And in her slightly inebriated state, she couldn't help but wonder if the misconceptions she'd been carrying about herself went beyond how other people perceived her. Laura had said that people viewed her better than she viewed herself.

And for the first time in a long time, Cara felt better. Better than better. She felt good.

And not just because her friend had said she looked great. The fact that she had so visceral a response to Rory's touch, to his close proximity, encouraged her to believe that maybe, just maybe, there was hope for her in other areas.

After all, if she could get such a high level of physical response from him simply holding her hand…?

Rory, being Rory, didn't let her stay silent for too long. He squeezed his long fingers around hers. 'What's going on in that mind of yours now? You've been silent as the grave since we left the club.'

Ooh, now, how to answer that one?

Her yellow streak jumped forwards. 'I was wondering about the ambush thing you were in.'

Rory's voice dropped an octave as he looked ahead of them, 'You don't want to wonder about that. Trust me.'

'Do you have family, Rory?'

The change in tack brought his eyes to hers, his dark brows folding down in momentary confusion. 'What?'

'Family.' She smiled up at him, tugged on his hand to keep his attention. 'You know, a mammy and a daddy, brothers and sisters. No. Hang on. I already know you have a brother. I guess I'm asking about the rest.'

His mouth quirked at her 'talk out loud' thought process. 'Yes. I have all of those things. Except the daddy. He died a few years back.'

'And what do they all think about you doing what you do? Don't they worry?'

'How did we end up talking about me?'

'Because you haven't asked me anything?'

She had him there. Again. So he smiled a fuller smile, his eyes sparkling in the dark light. 'How about we swap, then?'

'Onto me?' She shook her head in an exaggerated way. 'Uh-uh. I'm having way too much fun finding out about you.'

'I meant as in I tell you something, you tell me something.'

That took a moment or two's thought. But her curiosity about him had been growing for a while, and since the day in the street when he had awakened her to different ways of thinking about her body, she had been all the more curious about this complete stranger who seemed to know so well what she needed from him. And when.

Where had he come from? What was his life like? Why should he care what issues she had and want to help her overcome them?

Of the thousands of people that lived in Dublin, how had he managed to be in the right place at the right time?

She wanted to know. And in that moment, feeling better about herself than she had in years, walking along leafy streets hand in hand with a drop-dead gorgeous man, anything seemed possible. Even sharing.

'How about we swap like for like?'

'Same questions for both of us, you mean?'

'Yep.'

He smiled again. 'Are you always this cautious?'

'What sort of a question is that?' She smiled over at him. 'You're really bad at this game.'

Rory laughed. 'It's just that, rather than jump in with a barrage of questions like most women would, you feel the need to set the parameters before we start, which shows caution. So I was wondering if you're always this cautious. That's all.'

'Have we started yet?'

'Maybe.'

She smiled again at the teasing light in his dark eyes. 'Okay, then. Yes, I've always been this cautious. Well, since my teens anyway. We all have our own ways of dealing with things as we grow up. And you?'

'As in, am I cautious?'

'Uh-huh.' She smiled over at him. This wasn't so bad at all. In fact, it was pretty darn easy. See, she could do this. She could open up and let someone in….

'I'm cautious in my work, I have to be. And as I spend most of my time working, I guess, maybe, it spills over into other things.'

Cara nodded. That made sense.

But while she thought about it he bounded on in with another question, taking charge as he so often did, 'How long were you with your ex?'

Well, hell. That was what she got for not asking a safer question before he could think of one. Her immediate answer would have been 'too long' but she opted for the simpler truth, 'Four years.'

Rory's face turned towards hers, his eyes flickering with surprise. 'Really?'

'Yeah, I know, surprising and all as it may be that someone can put up with me for that long, right?' She laughed, swung their joined hands back and forth. 'I'm not the easiest to get along with, as you well know.'

His fingers tightened around hers for a second. 'That's not what I meant. It's just that four years is a pretty heavy commitment. Loads of people get married after less time than that.'

Cara felt a flush touching her cheeks. Again. He had an inherent habit of doing that to her. 'We nearly did.'

When she glanced up at him from the corner of her eye, she just had time to catch another flicker of surprise before he faced forwards again. 'So what happened?'

And there was the million-dollar question. She had asked herself that a hundred times. That was what people did after a breakup, after all. They looked at it, tore it apart at the seams, tried to analyze what had gone wrong so that, in theory, they could stop the same mistakes from happening all over again.

Thing was, she *knew* now. And it *so* couldn't happen again.

But she wasn't going to let introspective thoughts ruin the moment. Not this time.

'It just didn't work out.' And that was as close as she wanted to get to the nitty-gritty of it.

So she squeezed his fingers in return and tilted her head in his direction. 'Well, what about you? What's the longest you've lasted without running for the hills?'

'Lasted at what?' He glanced at her with a wicked grin on his face and waggling eyebrows, laughing when she rolled her eyes in response. 'Oh, you mean the relationship part?'

'Yes I mean the relationship part, oh he-of-the-one-track-mind. Like for like questions, remember?'

'It slipped my mind for a second.'

'I'll bet.' She smiled as they turned a corner and made their way along the street next to hers. 'Go on, then.'

He took a deep breath beside her. 'I'm not much for staying in one place for very long. I've told you that.'

'Yes, you have. Rather a lot, as it happens. So, you're Mr. Love-em-and-leave-em, huh?'

'That paints me in a bad light, don't you think?'

'Ah, you see, the truth hurts.'

He chuckled, and squeezed her fingers again. 'It's not that I haven't gone out with women. I just work a lot. There's not much point in asking someone to hang around waiting when I don't know where I'll be from one month to the next or for how long.'

'That's very thoughtful of you. I guess.'

Out of her peripheral vision she could see his face turn to hers, his voice low when he spoke again. 'It's just the way it is, that's all. That's why I wanted you to know from the start. I don't want to lie to you.'

'And you haven't, I don't think. Well, that's how it feels anyway.' She risked a glance up at him and smiled what she hoped was an encouraging smile. It had been so long since she'd used one on a man. Especially one she was so genuinely attracted to. Which she was. Amazingly.

Maybe she was finally making headway towards those changes in her life after all. Flirting openly with a man as hot as Rory was certainly a move in the right direction.

His fingers tightened again. 'It's important you know that.' He smiled wryly. 'And I have to admit it's been a while since I've felt the need to be this up front.'

Cara smiled while she thought about that, absent-mindedly letting her fingers thread in and out of his, letting herself notice the small pads of rough skin there and the differences in size between his and hers.

Rory was smiling a half smile at her when she glanced his way again, the light in his eyes dancing.

And she blushed in response. 'Don't do that.'

His short burst of laughter was a low rumble meant only for her ears. 'I can't smile at you?'

'Not like that, you can't.' She turned her face away from his, raising her chin indignantly as she focused on the path ahead of them, the street virtually deserted. 'You don't just smile. You *smile*.'

Rory continued smiling. 'And what exactly does that mean? A smile is a smile. It means I'm happy right this minute; it means I'm pleased to be in your company; it means I'm ecstatic we're not arguing. Surely those are all good things?'

'Oh-h-h—' she laughed the word out, glancing at him from the corner of her eye '—there's way more to that smile than that and you know rightly there is.'

'Like maybe the fact that I've noticed I have hold of your hand and you haven't snatched it back off me?'

Cara stopped dead and turned to face him, her head tilting while she batted her eyelids innocently. 'And you see that as a victory, do you? Like you've achieved something massively important just by holding my hand?'

'Haven't I?' He turned to face her, too, his head leaning towards hers as his voice lowered to an intimate grumble. 'Because, you see, I still have hold of it and you're still not pulling away, you haven't even thought up something sarcastic to say to try and push me away. I'd say that's a pretty big step in the right direction.'

Cara found herself mesmerized by the sparkle in his dark eyes. He really had the ability to look like the proverbial devil in disguise when he wanted to, and alone with him under the dim streetlights it should have had a zillion alarm bells going off in her head.

But he *did* still have hold of her hand. And she didn't want to think up something sarcastic to say to try and push him away. She *liked* that he had hold of her hand.

So, without answering, she resumed the gentle tangling of her fingers with his, which unleashed *that* smile again.

'You see—' he took another step closer '—you've done nothing but fight me off since day one, Cara Sheehan. And the fact that you're not fighting me now tells me something without you having to say it out loud.'

Her heart thundered so loudly in her chest she was sure he must be able to hear it. He was just so *intense.* So, so, sexy. And with her senses softened, her self-confidence at an all-time high, and her guard down...

She swiped her tongue across her mouth as her eyes dropped to the sensual curve of his. 'It's the alcohol. It makes people do things they normally wouldn't.'

The mouth she was studying curved into a smile again and she watched with fascinated eyes as his lips formed the words, his rumbling voice seduction itself.

'It lets people's guards down. Allows them to let go of some of the caution they normally carry around with them. Releases any inhibitions.'

'Yes.' Her answer was almost a whisper as her eyes rose to lock with his again. 'All of those things.'

And then she simply waited to see what he would do next. He could have no idea what it took for her to just stand there and do nothing, say nothing. What a major step it was, even with the relaxing effect of a little alcohol. She was by no means legless. No matter how weak her normally reliable knees felt right that minute. But her guard *was* definitely down.

Enough for her to wait and see what would happen when he figured out she wasn't offering *any* resistance.

Thing was, even while her heart continued to beat erratically and she could feel the heat build in her body and pool low in her abdomen, she still had the ability to think. Especially when he didn't make a move.

And while she thought, and waited, she knew that it wasn't just the alcohol that was allowing her guard down. It was because it was Rory. He'd already started to build her trust in him.

Silently she prayed that wasn't a mistake.

Thick, dark lashes fell and rose, once, twice, his gaze so hot it almost burned her eyes where it touched. 'If I had enough alcohol in my system to be where you are now, then I'd be kissing you right this minute.'

'You're saying you'd need to be drunk to kiss me?'

'I thought you said you weren't drunk?'

'I'm not. I'm…' she smiled a slow, purely sensual smile '…*relaxed and uninhibited.*'

Rory groaned and shook his head. 'You'd try the patience of a saint.'

That made Cara laugh. 'Oh, I think we're both aware of the fact you're no saint.'

'You're right, I'm not—' his voice dropped dangerously and he closed the last inch between their bodies, his fingers tightening on hers in warning '—but I won't have you using this against me tomorrow, either.'

Her head had to tilt farther back to keep the eye contact. 'We haven't done anything.'

'Not yet we haven't.'

They stood silently for a long, *long* time.

And Cara could feel it for the first time in her life. So this was that sexual tension thing, then. More than that even, because what this was had been building since the first day she'd laid eyes on him.

This was *anticipation.*

When she smiled in wonder at the realization, Rory shook his head again. 'What in hell made you think you weren't highly sexually charged? Let me tell you something—right now you have me burning up over here. And all we're doing is holding hands.'

As the question lingered in his eyes Cara pulled her gaze

away and looked down at their joined hands. Such a simple thing. The thing a human learnt to do before they even knew how to think cognitively.

A newborn baby would reach out for another human hand.

She reached their hands out to their sides, barely noticing the fact that his face had turned to look, too. Then she untangled her fingers, held her palm flat to his, watched as their fingers widened, tangled again, released and tangled again in the air beside them. She measured her smaller fingers against his, marvelled at the sight of how small and feminine her hand looked against his larger, broader male hand.

It was the most sensuous thing she had ever seen.

Her eyes rose to his at the same time as his rose to hers. And she smiled when he smiled.

Rory laughed. The rumble of it vibrating the air in the minuscule gap between their bodies. 'I may need to get you drunk more often.'

'I already told you. I'm not drunk.'

'But you're not stone-cold-sober, either. And when we do this, I want you to be completely aware it's happening.'

One arched brow quirked as her eyes focused again on his mouth. '*When?*'

'Yes Cara—' he ducked down until her eyes rose to meet his again '—*when*. It's been a question of when since you first walked through the door.'

It had? Through the dreamlike haze of sensuality Cara felt a tremor of fear.

What if it really was just the alcohol? What if Laura's earlier revelations had boosted her a little too far and she was now running onto new ground with a sense of confidence she really had no right to have?

There was just no way she could survive the world of hurt that would come from taking a chance again only to discover she had been right all along.

She stepped back, pulling her hand free of his.

Rory stepped forward again, his hand dropping to his side as he asked her in a soft voice, 'Why does that scare you so much?'

Oh, no. There they were. She could feel them in the backs of her eyes. The burning sensation that was a precursor of the familiar frustrated tears to come. And she just couldn't stand there in the middle of the street and cry in front of Rory. Of all the things she had fought so hard for over the years, her self-respect was the one she held dearest.

She just couldn't let go of that.

But when she tried to turn and run he was there, his large, solid frame blocking her path. She sidestepped, he stepped in front of her. She tried the other way, but his body was there in less than a second.

So she scowled up at him. 'Get out of the way, would you?'

'Not if it means you're gonna try running off, no.'

She looked from left to right. From neatly trimmed hedges behind wrought-iron fences to the one taxi that drove past them. Anywhere but back to the intense gaze she knew in her heart was right above her.

'I need to get home.'

'And I'm taking you home.' He stepped in again, his voice a husky temptation. 'Talk to me.'

'What do you want me to say?' Her voice crackled on the words and she had to swallow hard to dislodge the lump that had formed in her throat. This really wasn't fair. Just one time, would it be so very much to ask that he just quit and walk away?

'I want you to tell me why you're so scared of this. I want you, just once, to take a chance and talk to me honestly. No holding back, no being cautious, no starting an argument to avoid it, no worrying about what I might say tomorrow or thinking about how embarrassed you might feel when you next see me. Just say it out loud. And trust me.'

'No one does that, Rory. Not these days. We all hold something back.'

'And maybe by holding back we never get a chance to grow.

Maybe we miss out on what we might have learnt about ourselves by taking a chance.'

Her eyes locked with his. 'Said by the man who lays everything on the line about the things he feels and talks everything through freely? You can't tell me there aren't still things you hold back, too.'

Rory grimaced.

And Cara studied his face with wide, blinking eyes. Biting back her tears as she searched for a sign of him having more bravery than she did. And then she had a revelation. 'You really don't find it any easier to let me in than I do letting you in.'

He stared down at her for a long moment. 'And yet I find myself back here with you, talking to you, even when I've tried not to. Because you *fired* me.'

Suddenly it made a little more sense to her.

'Maybe because you know you'll never see me again after a while. And just once you want to know what it would be like to actually share more than the surface stuff with somebody? Maybe even because this arrangement of yours was as much for you as it was for me, but it was easier in your mind to make it for me?'

Maybe because he was at a point in his life where he needed time with her as much as she did with him?

'Maybe.'

The soft confession tore at her heart. Not fair, Rory Flanaghan. Seriously not fair. Making it something he needed made it more difficult for her to deny how much she needed.

'Don't you have friends or family that you can talk to about things?'

His dark brows rose in question. 'Don't you?'

'Not ones that I won't see again. Ones that I know I won't have to face knowing that they know things about me that I really *feel*. Things that I maybe worry they'll end up thinking less of me for when they know them. No.'

'Me, either. And considering that most of the friends I have are people who then have to trust their lives to me, it makes that a tad more difficult.'

Cara tilted her head towards her shoulder and swallowed hard. 'I don't have that to use as an excuse. So I guess you win.'

He raised his large hands and framed her face, his thumbs brushing against the corners of her mouth as she sighed breathily in response. 'It's not a competition that one or the other of us has to win, Cara.'

No, it wasn't.

She closed her heavy eyelids for a moment, allowing the sensation of his hands on her face to imprint itself on her memory for later reference.

Then she took a breath and opened her eyes. 'All right, you want a confession I'll give you one. I just don't know what I'm supposed to do about you and maybe that's why I keep fighting you off. You see, sometimes, like now, you just take my breath away.'

'And does that happen much with other men you meet?'

She frowned in confusion. 'The fighting them off or the breathless bit?'

'The breathless bit. Because it doesn't happen this much with me, either.'

It was no use. Fighting back her hot tears was a losing battle. As everything else with Rory seemed to be. But for the first time in a long time, it wasn't tears of bitterness. These tears came from deep inside, where a part of her felt as if it had just cracked open and a little of her soul had been set free. To soar.

The first drops formed in the bottom of her eyes, edged their way out onto her bottom lashes so that she had no choice but to blink and set them free onto her cheeks. But even as they fell she was smiling up at him.

'Thank you. That's good to know.'

Rory leaned his head closer, his words washing over her cheeks with his warm breath as his voice dropped. 'Let me help you see how wrong you are about yourself. Can you do that?'

Her answer was breathless, because she knew what he meant. She knew exactly what he meant. And the very idea of him trying to show her built a knot in her abdomen that almost doubled her over. But…

'What if I'm not wrong?'

'You are.'

She moaned when his mouth settled on hers. He had all the right words, knew what to say to her and when. As if he could see inside her and knew what she needed the most help with fixing. How was she supposed to keep fighting against that?

Rory was gentle at first, as if he was allowing her the opportunity to stop what was happening. But when he breathed out, she caught his breath and breathed it in, her body leaning into his in submission. So he let his hands drop from her face, and folded his arms around her waist, drawing her in against the familiar hard length of him.

She tilted her head, opened her mouth and met him touch for touch, taste for taste, her head spinning from the sensual assault.

Oh, yes.

While her body practically sang in response, she lifted her redundant hands, let them grip hold of his upper arms, allowing her fingers to flex against the muscles once before she walked them up along his shoulders, round his neck, until they found a home tangled in the hair at the nape of his neck.

Then her head tilted back a little and she let her tongue move with his. This was what they'd written about in magazines and romance novels, wasn't it?

This was what she'd been missing out on all this time. *Oh, Lord, yes.*

Rory dragged his mouth from hers and rested his forehead against hers, his breathing laboured. 'That's as far as I'm prepared to let this go right now, Cara. I meant what I said about you being sober enough to not hold this against me tomorrow. Just remember this. Whoever it was made you think less of yourself, or whatever doubts you had before now—you were *very* wrong.'

His throat convulsed as he swallowed. 'Because I've never met a woman I wanted this badly before.'

CHAPTER NINE

CARA WAS FLAT on her back, working her pelvis up and down against the Swiss Ball, when Rory interrupted the session.

There was only so much he could let another man watch while he watched him watching.

'I got it, Sam. Mrs McCauley is here for her three o'clock anyway.'

'You sure?'

Rory nodded an imperceptible amount. 'Go on ahead. I'll look after Cara.'

He stood tall until Sam said goodbye and left. Then he took a calming breath and hunched down beside Cara, his eyes focused on anywhere that wasn't her pelvis.

Professionalism, Flanaghan. *Remember?*

'And again, Cara.'

She pushed her feet in against the ball and lifted her pelvis again. And Rory gritted his teeth.

He could do this. He *could*.

Even while the only thing foremost in his mind was the way she'd felt in his arms when her body had submitted, her mouth had softened and her tongue had danced with his.

He could *be* professional, dammit!

'Another one.'

She thought she wasn't highly sexual?

'That's great. And again. Remember to pull in the abdominals as you push up.'

Rory made the mistake of looking at her face as her pelvis rose. Dark eyes locked with blue. And a crackle of pure electricity passed between them.

Big mistake.

Because even as her pelvis continued to rise and fall he had no point of focus beyond those eyes. And the questions they held.

Questions about the night before and what had happened between them. Had it been real? Had she felt what he'd felt? Had she wanted to make love as much as he had?

Nope. Hang on. Those were his questions. Which begged the question of what *she* was wondering.

Particularly about the lovemaking part.

'Hi.' It was all he could manage as he looked at her. She was truly the most distracting woman he had ever met.

'Hi.'

He noticed how, when she spoke, she sounded a little husky. As a result of the exercise, or because she was feeling what he was feeling? The quickening of pulse, the momentary loss of a steady heartbeat, the tension building low down inside?

Was he alone in all of that or did she feel it, too?

She was making him insane.

And not just because he'd had to have a cold shower when he went home—his first one in years as a solution for sexual tension.

Thing was, she was rapidly becoming more addictive a drug to him than the painkillers they had fed him when he'd come home. She was more of an ache in his chest than the throbbing pain in his leg had ever been. And there was no long-term fix for that beyond the obvious one.

Which he knew he couldn't rush. No matter how much he wanted to.

With her blue eyes fixed on his, she slowly raised her pelvis and dropped it again. As if it was an afterthought or some kind of reflex action while she focused on him. And with no obvious idea what the motion was doing to his libido. How could she *not* know?

He cleared his throat. 'You're doing great. Another half dozen.'

She wasn't even breathless when she spoke. A sign of her rising fitness level, he hoped, rather than a lack of the same sexual tension he was currently experiencing.

'Well, you got home okay, I take it.'

'Yep. No one mugged me along the way.'

'You could have taken them down with your good leg.'

Actually, he'd had enough repressed sexual tension to slay an army. 'Yep. That I could.'

And her pelvis rose and fell in slow motion.

So he cleared his throat again. 'How's your head doing today, then?'

Cara grinned beside him. 'Only hurts where the rabbit ears pinched it. I told you—' her grin faded to a smile that said volumes while her voice dropped '—I wasn't drunk. I knew what was happening. Just in case that's what you were worried about.'

Rory blinked as he looked down at her. He had to. In order to focus beyond the repetitive rise and fall of her pelvis. As a Team Leader in his work, it was his responsibility to be able to communicate clearly and succinctly. Cara Sheehan could take that away from him in a heartbeat.

What was with that?

Somewhere in the back of his mind, he knew it had to do with the rushed removal of the blood supply from his brain, *southwards.*

She continued, 'But for the record, I appreciate what you did.'

'Which part?' He smiled to ease the tension he felt.

When he waggled his eyebrows as he had the night before, she giggled. 'You can be such a moron when you want to be.'

'My kid sister tells me that all the time. I don't need you to do it, too.'

The statement brought them right back to where their conversation had started the last time he'd seen her. 'You have a kid sister?'

He nodded as her pelvis rose and fell. 'Yeah, she's seventeen and a real nuisance.'

'Still at school?'

He nodded again. 'We're aiming to have the youngest Flanaghan kids make it all the way past their exams and into higher education.'

Cara's arched brows rose in question. 'Meaning you didn't?'

'Meaning I did what I had to do to get into the army and that was that.' And Cara's pelvis rose and fell in his peripheral vision. 'I wasn't what you'd call academically orientated.'

'And yet here you are, an almost respectable businessman and owner of a city gym.'

'Three city gyms. In three cities. And half owner. I run them with my brother Connor, remember. Or, more to the point, he runs them while I'm not here. And we have another brother, Mal, doing weekends while he's at university.'

Her pelvis rose and fell. 'And you founded them all on the money you get from playing bodyguard?'

Rory gritted his teeth as he tried to keep concentrating on their conversation. 'Yes. And it's hardly a game. One more and then you can hit the pool.'

'How many of you are there?'

He could swear she made the last raise slower. Goddamn it. Did she have any idea he was hanging on by a thin thread over here?

'Six.' When she lowered her pelvis to the floor he exhaled. 'And you're done. Good job. I'll see you in the pool.'

'Six kids? Really?'

'Yes, six kids, really. And I got the privilege of being the eldest.'

'Any wonder you're so bossy most of the time.'

'What can I say? I was obviously born to it.' He resisted the urge to reach a hand out to help her up. Because he remembered what had happened the last time he had held her hand. And there was just no way he could let that happen in the middle of the gym's main floor.

See, he *could* be professional.

But he'd already checked that no one was booked into the pool. That cold shower of his had ruined any attempt at a good night's sleep. Which had given him time, alone in the dark, to think about how best to approach the dilemma of getting Cara to trust her body to him.

The pool had been pretty successful last time—to a certain degree. Lord knew he hadn't been able to forget about it!

Upright in front of him, Cara pulled one arm across her chest and stretched out her muscles the way he had taught her to. Which drew his eyes to her breasts.

She was wearing a vest top for the first time. A big improvement on the huge T-shirts she had been wearing up 'til now, in his humble opinion.

The vest top was tighter. The vest top wrinkled across her breasts as she changed arms and they squashed tighter together, creating the kind of cleavage that men went weak at the knees for.

Then she hesitated.

When he looked up into her eyes he saw a spark of something he hadn't seen before. And before his incredulous gaze her full mouth curved into a small smile and she stretched both arms above her head, leaned back a little, and sighed.

Which thrust her full breasts right back into his gaze again and drew a low, barely audible groan from deep in his throat.

When she giggled again he scowled at her and glanced around the room to see if anyone had noticed. Then he fixed her with a steely gaze. 'We're playing today, are we?'

'You were already looking. I just made it easier for you, is all.' She smiled a pert smile. 'You asked for it.'

'I think I liked you better when you were sarcastic.'

'Who said I'd stopped?'

With narrowed eyes he watched as she lifted her hand towel and flung it over one shoulder. 'Maybe I just decided last night it would be easier to play you at your own game rather than fighting you off. Not that I was having much success with that, anyway.'

Oh, really? Now he recognized what that spark in her eyes was. It was mischief. Whether or not she intended it as the flirtatious kind of mischief making was another matter. But it was what it looked like to him.

So he stepped closer, dropped his chin, his eyes still fixed on hers. 'That's a dangerous ploy, Ms Sheehan.'

Cara faltered.

And he smiled at her. 'But I'm *up* for whatever you can dish out. *Trust me.*'

Her gaze dropped to the front of his sweat pants, then rose, blue eyes wide with awareness.

Which made him chuckle. 'Go hit the pool. I'm gonna go check everything's okay out here before I head in.'

'Like *that?*'

'Honey—' he leaned his head closer and whispered '—not everyone is looking there.'

'It's tough to miss.'

'Well, it's your fault.'

A frown creased her forehead. 'I'm not sure how I feel about that being my fault.'

'Most women would be pretty proud.'

'I'm not most women.'

'Now *that* I'm only too well aware of. I don't actually walk around like this all the damn time.'

Her mouth quirked and her chin rose. 'Okay. I might actually be a little flattered by *that.*'

And he smiled back. *'Pool.'*

He took for ever joining her. Cara knew, because she had done laps to keep her occupied while she waited. And to keep her mind focused on anything that wasn't the distinct tent in the front of his sweat pants.

Or the almost painful expression on his face as he tried to control it before leaving her.

Which she was actually quite proud was her fault. Perverse female that she apparently was.

'Sorry.' He appeared through the door from the men's changing area. 'I had to talk to a couple of people.'

Cara continued to pull herself through the water, even though her arms were beginning to ache and her pulse had hitched at the sight of him. 'No problem. You have twenty to catch up on, just so you know.'

She could hear the smile in his voice without looking across to confirm it was there. 'Well, I better hurry up, then.'

There was a splash and the water rippled around her as he caught up. As her hand reached out for the tiles she tensed, prepared herself for his touch. Because that was what she'd been waiting for, wasn't it?

She hadn't been able to think about anything else since he had walked her to her door and backed away with *that* smile on his face.

Leaving her alone and more frustrated than she'd ever been in her entire life.

But as she turned round and stretched her arms out on either side of her head, he disappeared under the water, executed a perfect turn, and powered away.

Which made her frown.

Because she was then left to watch as he cut through the water with sleek arcs of his arms, the water glistening on his tanned skin.

Well, this wasn't going the way she'd thought it would, was it?

She let her legs play back and forth as he got close to her again. Tilted her head from side to side to ease the knot of tension building in her neck and prepared herself for his approach.

Only for him to make another turn and swim away.

He changed his stroke from crawl to breast-stroke halfway down his return lap and grinned, flashing white teeth at her.

'You finished swimming?'

'I'm twenty ahead, remember?'

His dark head tilted for a moment. 'True.'

He made another turn, so she called across to his back. 'I'll just wait here 'til you catch up, then.'

'Whatever you fancy, hon.'

Cara scowled at his back. Well, this wasn't at all what she'd thought it would be like when they were next alone. He had said 'when' last night. And by the time he had rested his forehead against hers after the best kiss of her life, she had pretty much resigned herself to the fact that there was going to be a 'when'. Her night-time meanderings of the mind had even thought that might not be an entirely bad thing. It was time for her to try.

And he was a perfect candidate.

He obviously had more of an effect on her body than any other man ever had. And he wasn't giving up. So maybe just allowing it to happen, to see whether or not he was right when he had said she was wrong about her sex drive, wouldn't be such a bad idea after all.

And if she wasn't wrong, then he couldn't say he hadn't been warned.

Not twenty minutes ago he had been turned on. Big time. And having been almost burned alive by his heated gaze, she was more than ready herself. It had to have been written all over her face.

So what the hell was going on?

She'd have folded her arms across her breasts and pouted if she hadn't thought she would sink like a stone.

Men!

Rory was on his way back again. 'So, now that you know all about my family, why don't you tell me about yours?'

If she wasn't already in a mood, then talking about her family would put her there. He wanted to make small talk *now?* Terrific.

'What do you want to know?'

'You have brothers and sisters?'

'Stepsisters. Two of them. My dad remarried after my mum died when I was nine.'

'That must have been tough.' He waited for a moment before making his turn, treading water in front of her. 'Do you get on with your new mum?'

'She's okay. She tries hard. But she's not my mother.'

Rory nodded, then swam forwards and made his turn. 'You're close to your dad, though, I'll bet?'

'Yes. I've never outgrown being his little girl. My stepsisters hated that about me when we were all teenagers. But from my point of view, they had nothing to complain about when they looked the way they did.'

Pulling her gaze away from the tempting sight of his muscled back, Cara scowled at the ceiling instead. Great. Here she'd been all set up for some experimental playing around and instead she was dragging up the pathetic story of her teenage angst. Perfect.

And all too typical of her life, really.

So much for bloody anticipation.

'Do you have a fairy godmother, too?'

With a loud sigh she dropped her head back onto the tiles and let her legs float upwards. 'Now there's one I haven't heard before.' She heard the splash of him making his turn at the opposite end. 'Because they didn't throw that old chestnut at me every five minutes when there was an audience. And it was *so* much funnier when the ugly sisters weren't ugly and good old Cinders here was a beach ball with fingers.'

She puffed her cheeks out and waggled her fingers up off the tiles. Unaware he was watching until there was a burst of familiar male laughter.

'It can't have been as bad as you thought it was.'

Cara snorted as gracefully as she could manage to, tilting her chin onto her chest to look at him. 'Well, we've already established *your* rare liking for females who *curve*. But trust me when I tell you there weren't too many guys around with the same liking when I was growing up. Not with the perfect twins around. Both five eight, both naturally slim, both blond and—' she pursed her lips and shook her shoulders '—*perky*. If I hadn't been such a porker I'd have been invisible.'

He was barely holding back a devilish grin. '*Twins?*'

'O-kay. We're done here, I think.' With a kick of her legs she turned round and leaned the palms of her hands on the tiles to pull herself out.

Her first attempt failed. And the added frustration of it drew a colourful expletive from her mouth.

Then the water moved behind her and a warm, hard chest was pressed against her back. His hands gripped either side of her waist to hold her in place as his mouth hovered inches above her neck and he spoke in a husky grumble.

'Oh, we're not done here. Not by a long chalk.'

CHAPTER TEN

CARA GASPED AS Rory continued. 'Not when I just had to tell three people we were having the pool cleaned today.'

His mouth touched the column of her neck, his tongue darting out to sweep the pool water from her skin in an upwards motion before he whispered in her ear, 'So I could make certain we didn't get interrupted.'

She gasped again as he moved behind her, using the hands on her waist as an anchor while he formed a seat for her to perch on with his legs. Bringing her rear into direct contact with the hard ridge of an impressive erection.

So she grumbled at him in a husky voice, 'Well, you weren't in any hurry to jump all over me when you got here.'

His mouth curved into a smile against the sensitive skin behind her ear. 'And miss seeing you as frustrated as I've been since the last time we were in this pool? I don't think so.'

Cara attempted to squirm away. But all that did was rub her rear across his erection again, before it settled, long and hard, right against where she would most like it to be. And she had to bite her bottom lip to stop herself from moaning aloud.

Instead she let her legs dangle off either side of his thighs, her back arching forward as he nuzzled behind her ear again. Which in turn thrust her breasts forward in a reflex action, drawing her attention to how heavy they felt, how tight the wet material of her swimsuit suddenly felt against them.

If he was going to touch her then why didn't he just touch her already? He'd been plenty drawn to them earlier. And she would *not* beg!

'You can ask me, you know.'

She swallowed hard to damp her throat enough to speak. 'Ask you what?'

Was that breathless voice really hers? Man, she could be quite the little sex kitten in the right pool with the right man, couldn't she?

She giggled. As much out of sudden embarrassment as amusement at the thought of herself as a sex kitten.

'To touch you where you want to be touched.'

Terrific. Now he could read minds. 'You know where I want you to touch me.'

'I want you to tell me.'

She giggled again, almost a little hysterically. 'I don't think I can actually do that out loud. Why don't you just take a wild guess?'

Rory shifted behind her, his entire body stiffening as her rear moved again. He lifted a hand from her waist and gripped the tiles to steady them, then held his other palm up in front of her. 'How about you show me?'

Cara hesitated. Show him? Take hold of his hand and put it on her where she wanted it to be? *Everywhere* she wanted it to be? Oh, dear Lord.

She wasn't sure he had enough hands.

But she knew what he was doing. He was, quite literally, handing the control over to her. She could stop him if she wanted to; she could play it safe and put his hand on her cheek or back on her stomach, or she could put it on one of her aching breasts. It was her call.

It was also her opportunity to grasp what he was offering her. He was offering her patience, which in his present state of rampant arousal couldn't be an easy thing for him to do. He was offering her silent understanding that the very fact she'd even let them get this far without a fight was a big step for her.

He was offering her his expertise to try and get over the one major issue she still carried about: her own sexuality.

And he was allowing her to let loose a side of herself she'd kept buried all of her adult life.

He was the most amazing man she'd ever met.

Lord, how she wanted him!

And if she hadn't known he would walk out of her life before too long, she might even have allowed herself to fall for him a little.

But he *would* be gone. And she'd never have the embarrassment of seeing him on the street somewhere knowing what they had done. No matter what they did.

So she swallowed again and lifted one hand off the tiles to lay it palm to palm with his.

He tangled his fingers with hers as they had the night before, turned his hand over so that it was under hers, his deep voice rumbling against her ear. 'Show me.'

Her fingers arched over the indentations of his finger joints, fingertips rising and falling over his knuckles. Then she curved them around the edges of his hand and lifted, hesitating for a split second an inch above her breast. Before she arched forwards into his palm and sighed breathily as his fingers curved around the aching weight.

'Here, Cara?'

She exhaled her answer. 'Yes.'

Rory pushed his knees in against the side of the pool, water sliding over their bodies as he moved his fingers over the curve of her breast.

Her hand automatically lifted from his to reach for the tiles; she needed something to *grip*. But he grumbled at her, 'No. Keep your hand there. Then you can guide me.'

He hoisted her more securely on his lap so she was forced to grip his hand tighter, increasing the pressure of his fingers on her breast and drawing a low, earthy moan from her lips.

'See.' He smiled against her neck. 'I told you that curves were sexier.'

When her head dropped back against his shoulder he pressed his lips against her temple and she smiled a soft smile in return.

It was an incongruous act considering what they were doing. One that spoke of a tenderness in him that she should already have had a hint of. It had been there the night before when he had been so careful not to push her too far in her 'relaxed' state, had been there in the warmth of his dark eyes as he'd left her at her door.

He made her feel *cared for.*

Which she instinctively rewarded with more open honesty.

'I can't remember ever having felt sexier than I do right this minute.'

'Thank you. That was the general idea.'

His fingers moved again, brushing back and forth on her breast until he was rewarded by the tightening of her nipple beneath the wet material. He bent a finger, flicked his short nail back and forth over the tip.

And she moaned again, squirmed on his lap again.

Which in return drew a low, rumbling groan out against her cheek before he brushed a hint of coarse stubble over her smooth skin.

'Swap hands.'

The water lapped around them and up over the tiles as they adjusted their bodies and swapped their hands so that he could touch her other breast. And Cara sighed in satisfaction.

'Good?'

She laughed huskily. 'Hell, yes.'

'Tell me what you're feeling.'

'I'm aching.'

'Where?'

'Everywhere.'

'What kind of an ache? Tell me.'

A hollow ache; one that had centred low in her abdomen and was building a throbbing knot of tension inside her. She could feel it radiating out along her nerve endings, up into her tingling breasts, down over the taut muscles in her thighs, centering in the core of her; where she burned from the friction of his erection against her.

'I'm aching inside.' Her breasts rose and fell in deep, shuddering breaths.

He flicked his thumbnail over her distended nipple and demanded in a husky voice, 'Show me where.'

It was easier to follow the instruction the second time around. Now that she knew how good it felt, she wanted more, needed more.

She swallowed again, parted her lips as she breathed, closed her eyes as her head got heavier against his shoulder. Then guided his hand downwards, his fingers curling underneath her breast, tracing each rib as she gasped inwards, before they spread wide over her belly, almost possessively.

When his palm was resting low on her abdomen she squeezed his fingers with hers and sighed, 'Here.'

'And here.' The tip of his smallest finger brushed against her pubic bone.

It was a statement of fact rather than a question. But she answered him anyway. 'Yes, there most of all.'

It was the most blatant invitation she could have issued him beyond crying out for him to take her there and then. Which it was on the tip of her tongue to do.

She was his for the asking.

But rather than accepting the invitation he turned his hand over and tangled his fingers with hers, while he turned his head and kissed her arched neck again. His lips stilling against her skin, she had to strain to hear his whispered words.

'You're killing me, woman.'

Cara smiled, opened her eyes, and turned her face towards his, forced to lift from his shoulder a little to see him. And when he opened his eyes and focused his dark gaze on her she melted against him. 'That goes both ways.'

Rory watched her long lashes blink at him for the longest time. Then tightened his fingers around hers and frowned.

'And, much as I'm sorely tempted to just keep going, we're gonna stop now.'

They were? When she'd just offered her body up on a silver platter?

He wasn't the only one frowning.

'And why is that, exactly?'

His expression softened at the sound of the frustration in her voice. 'Believe me when I say it's not because I want to stop.'

'Then why are you? In case you hadn't noticed, *I'm* not stopping you.'

Dragging his eyes from hers, he looked heavenwards as he took a deep breath that pressed his naked chest tighter against the naked skin on her back. 'Because I'm not going to make love to you in a swimming pool. Tempting as that may be. Not right this minute.'

'You told everyone it was being cleaned—' she smiled impishly when his gaze flickered back to her face '—and I thought we were already making love.'

Rory shook his head, very slowly, his eyes fixed on hers again. 'No. This isn't making love. This is just foreplay.' He smiled a slow smile. 'In fact, it barely makes it into the league of foreplay.'

'You *think?*'

'No. I *know.*' Untangling his fingers from hers, he dropped his knees and pushed back from the pool edge, so that Cara was left floundering for a moment. Then treading water a little away from her, he waited for her to turn round and stare at him with large eyes filled with the same need he felt.

'When we make love, Cara, I want to hear you cry out. And that can't happen in here while there are people outside who can hear. I won't do that to you; I won't let you ever feel ashamed of what you feel with me. I want you to know how wrong you've been about yourself.' He smiled a half smile. 'You already sense it, don't you?'

Cara could feel her throat constricting as she stared back at him; could feel the heat in the back of her eyes again. Did he have any idea how amazing he was?

She nodded. 'Yes.'

'We're going to take this real slow. Until neither of us can take any more. *Then* we'll make love. I promise you.' He smiled. 'Do you trust me?'

'Yes, I trust you.'

And she knew she did. She just had to trust herself not to get involved any deeper emotionally than she already was; to have enough strength to give her body without giving away her heart.

'Okay, then. Be ready at seven.'

Cara was ready *now*. But already she could feel a thrill at the thought of what was ahead of her. 'What have you got planned for seven?'

'Ah, now. That would be telling.'

CHAPTER ELEVEN

'NICE CAR.'

Cara watched as Rory's broad chest puffed a little with pride. 'She's my baby. Though if there was a hotline for neglected cars to phone, she'd be on it loads.'

Cara glanced at her much loved Mini where it was parked in front of the sleek lines of the dark BMW. It was a more practical car for the city, she told herself. It was easy to park, cheap to run. Cute. Whereas *this* car…

She ducked her head down as he opened the door, her eyes taking in the spotless interior and the over-abundance of leather upholstery.

This car was all male.

No tiny bear on the dashboard, no crumpled receipts in the side pockets. No half-eaten packet of crisps on the passenger seat or spare lipstick below the gearstick.

Rory stepped a little closer to her, his hand still on the open door as he looked inside. 'What?'

'She certainly looks neglected. You can tell you're not in it much from the lack of *stuff.*'

He laughed. 'What can I say? Years in the army will teach you to be tidy.'

He was *so* never going inside her house.

Cara stood upright again and turned to look at him. She hadn't lied when she'd told him there were times when he took her breath away. And if he'd looked good on her porch, then out on the street basked in the evening summer sunshine he looked *yum*.

And all he was wearing was jeans and a dark V-necked sweater. Cara practically salivated.

Her eyes focused on the hint of hair at the apex of the V, and her abdomen tightened in response. Oh, this was really getting silly. Not that long ago she'd had control over her body; now she was ragingly turned on by body hair.

So she forced herself to look up into his eyes. 'Where are we going?'

'Out.'

'Out where?'

He flashed even white teeth at her. 'Now where's your sense of adventure?'

'In a swimming pool at your gym, I think.'

In an instant he was around the open door and had placed a firm kiss on her mouth, his voice low. 'That's my girl. Now get in the car.'

Cara found herself unable to stop grinning like an idiot. This flirting thing was fun. Being taken on a mystery tour was definitely fun. Getting kissed on a summer's evening by a terrifically sexy man? Fun, fun, fun.

Yep, the whole changing things in her life was going rather well, as it happened.

So she did as she was told and folded herself into the interior of the car, immediately cocooned in sensual scents of leather and familiar cinnamon.

With the door quietly clicking closed beside her, she got to watch with appreciative eyes as Rory strode round the bonnet and slid onto the seat beside her. He even *moved* sexily.

'Your limp is better.' Her smile faded at the realization. If he was getting better then he was getting closer to leaving, wasn't he?

Rory grinned at her as he buckled his seat belt. 'Yep, it most definitely is. Must be all that swimming.'

Cara settled her back against the door as she looked down at his long legs. 'Did the bullet go through it?'

'Nope. It bounced around the armour-plating of the Jeep some before it found a place to get stuck. So there wasn't enough force left to send it through.' He twisted his lean body towards her as he looked over his shoulder to back the car out. 'I was lucky. A through and through would have bled like a bugger.'

She didn't actually believe it was all that lucky. *Not* being shot; now *that* was lucky. But then she thought about his friend and it made her realize that, from Rory's point of view, he *had* been lucky. If his friend was anything like he was, then his journey would be a rough one. It would be for anyone.

'Was the friend you visited in the same car?'

'Rich?' His face darkened briefly as he frowned; the way it always did at the mention of his friend's name. Then he glanced at her for a second as he faced forward again, turning the car onto the road. 'No. He was in the other vehicle. We'd dropped off the construction crew and were heading home to wait 'til they needed collecting. His vehicle was in front of mine. They wait until they have you both roughly the same distance away from the charge before they hit you, you see, to try and get you both at the same time. Rich's was just closer was all.'

Cara went silent beside him as his words sank in. He had said it all in such a matter-of-fact tone. As if they'd been driving down the motorway and been in a bit of a bump. But he knew Cara was no idiot, not in everything anyway, so he had to know she would put it all together.

He glanced briefly across at her. 'You okay?'

She took a short breath. 'You said you'd been shot. You never said anything about being blown up.'

'Possibly because you barely believed I'd been shot?'

This time when he glanced at her he even had the gall to grin. When what they were talking about wasn't even the least bit funny. When he had first told her it had been different; she hadn't trusted him then. His story of being shot had been as real to her as a fairy godmother had been when she was growing up.

She had thought that generally he was full of—

Now was different. Now she knew him better. Now she was in a relationship, *of sorts,* with him.

And she cared.

'Do they try to blow you up often? Or was that a special occasion?' If he could be so calm about it, then she could play that game, too, even while her stomach somersaulted at the thought of something happening to him.

Thing was, she suddenly knew she would still feel that way even when he was gone. Every news report she caught a glimpse of on the TV wouldn't seem as if it were a million miles away any more. She knew she would end up straining to see the faces of the people who were hurt, would feel the fear until a list of names was announced.

Because, realistically, if anything ever did happen, not only would there be nothing she could do about it. She also wouldn't have the right to find out the end result. Who would she ask? Who would think she needed to be told?

She was nobody to the people he cared about, the people who *would* be told. All she was, realistically, was another passing affair; one of many he must have had before her, no doubt.

And that was part of the reason he didn't get involved with women, wasn't it? The realization was as clear as day to her. He wouldn't intentionally put someone else through all that.

The dark wool of his sweater rose and fell as he shrugged, his face turning away from hers as he pulled the steering wheel and negotiated through the traffic. 'It happens the odd time. The local guys normally check the roads out. But every now and again they miss one.'

'You talk about it like it's just another day at the office.'

'It is.' He smiled her way again. 'We all knew what we were doing when we got into it. And that's the reason we get paid so well. I couldn't do the things I've done at home if it wasn't for the job.'

'And is that why you do it? For the money?'

'Well, I sure as hell wouldn't be doing it without the money. But at the start I guess there was a bit of a rush with it, too. Every boy wants to play the action hero at some point and my time in the army didn't exactly fulfil that fantasy for me. Ireland isn't famous for getting into scraps. But the training I got there stood me in good stead for what I do now. And I happen to think the little people have the right to do their job and earn a wage. We help them do that. It's not about taking sides. Not for me.'

Cara mulled over the abundance of information, turning to look forwards out of the tinted windscreen. It hadn't escaped her that the bond of trust they had initiated in the pool earlier seemed to have opened them up to trusting each other with more personal information. And without any great difficulty, either; as if a barrier had been removed.

She just wasn't convinced she needed to know as much as she now did.

But it was all part and parcel of the complex puzzle that was Rory Flanaghan. The man whom pretty soon she would share a bed with. And she just wasn't the kind of woman who could do that with someone she didn't know better.

Still focused on his driving, Rory didn't seem to notice her silence.

'Then there are the lads, of course. When you do the job for a while you get pretty close. So, after a while, it's not just for yourself or the workers that you do it. It's for them, too. You learn to rely on each other. Quitting means they get some new wet-behind-the-ears pup who might not react as quick. I couldn't do that to them, not now. Especially not now.'

'The army probably taught you to think like that, too.' Her response came out almost on its own, her voice a dull monotone.

'Yeah, that and being the eldest kid; I've had people to look out for all my life.'

As he was now doing with her.

She turned her face towards him again. Beneath all the layers of testosterone and alpha male behaviour, he was a caring, giving man.

Her eyes roamed over his dark hair, past the forehead covered with strands of fringe, along the nose that had the slight bump on the bridge, lingering on the sensual curve of his slightly wider lower lip until she traced the strong line of his jaw back up to his eyes.

At the exact moment he turned and looked at her.

His eyes sparkled in amusement. 'What now?'

He glanced back at the road, then back at her face.

And Cara smiled affectionately in response. 'Oh, I have you sussed now, Flanaghan.' She made an exaggerated nod and leaned back on her seat, arms crossed. 'Yes, indeed-y. No fooling me. You're a *nice guy.*'

He grimaced beside her. 'Ouch.'

'Uh-huh. You just have to suck it up and face facts.'

As the car made a turn onto a narrower road and the ocean came into view at their side, Rory reached a hand over to take one of Cara's hands from her lap. Then, hands joined, he used them to change gears before he leaned closer and leered.

'You might not think that if you knew what I had in mind for later.'

She laughed, her body heating as her imagination took flight. 'Nope. It's no good. The truth's out now. Your secret is a secret no longer.'

A set of traffic lights turned red in front of them and Rory slowed the car down, the engine purring as it rested. And with a sensuous smile he leaned closer and claimed her mouth, his firm lips moving over hers in a way that clearly staked a claim and branded her with a heated promise. Leaving her in no doubt of what he had in mind for 'later'.

A horn sounded behind them and he tore his mouth away, their joined hands changing gear before he moved the car forward. 'Nice guys don't think about ravishing women on the front seat of a car on a public road.'

Cara couldn't help but laugh again. It was how she felt was all. A bubble of happiness inside her chest that she couldn't remember having felt demanding to be freed. It was as simple as that.

But he wasn't long in putting a flush onto her cheeks as he glanced sideways at her again and informed her in a deep voice, 'Have I mentioned how glad I am you're wearing a skirt, by the way? Makes things much easier. Tell me you're not wearing any underwear and you'll fulfil a fantasy or two, as well.'

She did the only thing she could think of and punched his forearm with her free hand.

And he laughed in return. 'See, not that nice a guy after all.'

'Where are we going, you moron?'

'Dun Laoghaire. We're going to eat so you can keep your strength up. For *later.*'

Cara blinked across at him. But when she looked past his profile, she could already see the harbour ahead and the familiar sight of a ferry sailing out for Wales.

So she remained silent for most of the trip while Rory changed gears with her hand.

It was only as they pulled into the tiny streets behind the harbour and he looked for a parking space that he spoke again. 'I've been looking at a place to buy round here and found this great place to eat.'

Cara glanced across at him again, her eyes wider. 'You've been looking for a house *here?*'

He nodded. 'Yeah, its close enough to the city and it seems like a nice enough place to live. I needed to think about a place to buy rather than kipping on Connor's spare bed every time I'm home. The amount of time I've been home this time has shown me we both need our own space. I thought I'd rent out a room or two so there's someone there while I'm away.'

'That makes sense—' she glanced up and down the small street, having to turn round in her seat to see all the way back '—but there are loads of good areas to choose from.'

'True. But I found one here I like in my price range.'

Cara grimaced slightly as he found a space and slid the car into it. He just would find one here.

'There's loads of history here, too. I quite like that. Did you know it used to be called Kingstown? They didn't change it back 'til the nineteen twenties.'

'Uh-huh.' As she unclipped her seat belt she looked up and down the street again. 'I'd heard that.'

He squeezed her hand before he released it, which drew her eyes up to his face. 'You okay?'

Cara forced herself to smile at his quizzical expression. 'I'm starving. Where's this place, then?'

'It's just down the street.'

'Terrific. Let's go.'

He took her hand as they walked along, which was now so familiar an act that she barely noticed it. Mind you, she was still looking around her, eyes darting back and forth. And she didn't breathe properly until they had ducked down below the low doorway and made their way into the low ceilinged basement restaurant.

Then she smiled up at him as they sat down. *Made it.*

'Cara?'

She closed her eyes and groaned. 'Oh, hell.'

When she opened them, Rory's dark eyebrows rose in question. 'You know people here?'

'You could say that.'

'Darling, it is you! I said it was you. But the light is so low in here that your dad didn't believe me. You know what his eyes are like these days. And he said you'd have phoned if you were popping down.'

Cara was still looking at Rory's bemused expression when her stepmother stopped at the side of their table. She tilted her head and sighed, smiling upwards. 'Mother, this is Rory; Rory, my stepmother Joyce.'

They were shaking hands when her dad appeared and kissed

her cheek. 'This is a lovely surprise, sweetheart. You should have called.'

'And my Dad; James.'

'James and Joyce,' Joyce giggled. 'Like the writer, you know? It's a little joke in the family.'

Rory nodded slowly, a vague look of incredulity on his face. 'You come down to Dun Laoghaire often?'

'Oh, no, dear.' She patted his arm. 'Didn't Cara mention it? We live just up the road. Have done for eighteen years; since we got married.'

Rory quirked a dark brow at Cara. 'This is where you're *from?*'

With her lips pursed in resignation she nodded slowly.

'How funny she didn't mention it. Oh, yes, we're only a few minutes walk from here, on Whitworth Street.'

Rory grinned at Cara briefly before turning the charm on Joyce. 'Yeah, I know it. I just put in an offer on a house there.'

'Oh, how wonderful!' Joyce clapped her hands. 'You must come over and join us for dinner. There are extra seats at our table. Isn't this just lovely, James?'

CHAPTER TWELVE

'I'M A BIT confused.'

Cara sighed at Rory's side. 'I didn't know where you were taking me. It was your idea to make it a magical mystery tour.'

'I'm not confused about that part. But you could have mentioned something when you knew where we were going.'

'Yes, I could. But I didn't want to ruin it with a hissy fit and I hoped this was their bridge night.' She scuffed her toe against some loose gravel. 'Believe me when I say that doing the "meet the parents thing" was the last thing on my mind when you picked me up tonight.'

Rory smiled at the small pout on her mouth. 'They're nice, surprisingly enough.'

Her chin rose and he smiled even more when she frowned at him. 'Of course they're bloody well nice. Who said they weren't?'

No one had. He'd just kind of assumed it. All Cara's complexes about herself had to come from somewhere, after all. And after the things she had said in the pool earlier he had assumed it wasn't all the slug-like ex, that maybe she'd had a tough time growing up.

Now that he'd done the 'meet the parents thing', he knew she couldn't have had that tough a time there. They had money; he now knew her father was a property developer, which had led to a long discussion about the best renovations Rory could make on his new house. And her stepmother was witty and charming, both things Rory happened to be good at, so he'd got on with her like a house on fire, too. It was only Cara who had been hard to pull into the conversation.

Maybe the twins were the problem? Though if they were anything like the rest of the family he couldn't see that being the reason, either…

He had a sudden image of Cara's expression when she'd said they were 'perky', and he laughed aloud, which promptly turned Cara's frown into a dark scowl.

She shook her head at him and walked faster along the seafront. But he caught her in one long stride and reached for her hand.

The hand she snapped away.

Ruining his good mood sharpish. 'What in hell is wrong now?'

'Nothing's wrong! You just said my parents were nice. And it was pretty bloody obvious they *adored* you.'

'And yet you're now having a—what did you call it?' He stepped in front of her and looked up into the night sky for the words before fixing her with an impassive gaze. '*Hissy fit.* Is there something wrong with them adoring me? I happen to think I'm pretty bloody adorable.'

She faltered, opened her mouth to say something, threw an arm out to the side, and then finally spat out, 'There's not much point in them thinking you're adorable.'

'There is when we're gonna be neighbours.'

'You won't be there long enough to be classed as a neighbour.'

'And you're worried that might hurt your parents' feelings?'

'No!' Her eyes flashed in the dim light. 'I'm just for evermore going to be reminded of how bloody adorable you are and what a failure I am that there's no one like you permanently in my life!'

When her eyes widened he knew she had said more than she'd meant to in the heat of the moment. But he also now knew her well enough to know when she wasn't done. So he took a breath and looked around.

Then he looked back at her and stretched an arm out, index

finger pointing. 'I'm going to sit down on that wall over there and you're going to explain that to me. That way we'll get rid of any more confusion.'

She smirked at him in response.

And even though he wanted to shake her for being so stubborn, or kiss her silly—which was what he had wanted to do all the way through dinner—he resisted and stepped over to the wall. Where he sat down, spread his legs wide, and folded his arms across his chest.

And waited.

She stood side on to him for a long time, her head tilted back.

So he studied his feet for a while, looked over his shoulder at a returning ferry. And eventually took a long breath. 'Just whenever you're ready. No rush.'

'I hate you.'

'No, you don't. You just hate me right now.'

Cara laughed sarcastically. 'You have no idea how much.'

'Well, I'm sitting over here with my bum going numb waiting to hear whatever it is you have to tell me, so you go right on ahead and tell me how much. Shoot from the hip, woman. I can take it.'

She turned her head and glared at him. 'It has nothing to do with you!'

'Well, what does it have to do with, then?'

'It has to do with me.'

'And that just means I want to know all the more.'

He wasn't entirely sure, but he could have sworn she growled at him.

Then she lifted her arms in a shrug of surrender and began to pace back and forth in front of him. The sea breeze caught her long skirt and plastered it in against her legs, the material hugging her thighs. When she turned it flared out, curled back in and perfectly outlined her rear, with no visible panty line. And Rory had to swallow hard and force himself to concentrate.

'I'm ready when you are.'

It took two more rows of pacing before his patience was rewarded.

'I really wanted to hate Joyce when I was little, but she was so bloody nice I just couldn't. And my dad loved her so much—'

'Still does, from what I could see.'

'Even when he finds it tough most of the time to get a word in edgeways.'

Rory smiled. He'd noticed that.

'And the twins are exactly like her, you know.'

She stopped in front of him as she said it and he held back a smile and answered, 'Yes. You mentioned that earlier. *Perky.*'

'Exactly!' She started pacing again. 'And let me tell you, going from a quiet household to all that ruckus wasn't easy. They were everywhere, giggling and chattering away and swapping clothes. And all I could do was watch.'

'You were *quiet?*' He knew that his expression probably gave away the fact he had difficulty believing that.

'Yes.' She glared at him enough for him to know he'd been caught. 'I know that's probably hard for you to believe, but I was. And I was a loner. And bookish. And I had glasses, for crying out loud!'

'And carried a few extra pounds of puppy fat, you said.'

'Would you like me to lie down so you can kick me?'

'Honey, if you lie down, kicking you is the last thing I'll be doing.'

'How can you possibly be turned on by that image? No other boy within shouting distance ever was before.'

Rory unfolded his arms and rested his palms on the wall on either side of him. 'Is that when you grew a complex about yourself?'

She hesitated, frowning hard as she looked down the pathway.

And Rory could almost feel the inner conflict in the air. She was fighting a battle. The loner teenager still buried inside her and unwilling to share.

The urge to stand up and fold her in his arms was so strong that he almost had to sit on his hands to stop it happening. She had an inherent ability to pull his protective nature to the fore. As if a part of her was invisibly willing him to reach out and make her pain of old disappear.

But she was a different woman now from the teenager she'd been back then. She was a fighter. Whether she chose to believe she was or not. The evidence had been there from the beginning in the way she would fend him off at every step. Rory had never met a woman who had made him work so hard to get her.

Or made him *want* to fight that hard.

'*Yes.*' The word was almost whispered, was said on a sigh that told him it was practically the confession of a lifetime for her. 'And Niall didn't help any, either.'

Rory's breath caught in his chest, a wave of anger so strong washing over his body that he could have punched something there and then.

'*Go on.*'

Cara heard the edge to his voice and glanced his way, her eyes running over the tense set of his shoulders and the tight line of his jaw before she looked into his eyes.

So Rory forced himself to take a breath, made his voice soft. 'Tell me what he did.'

She blinked back at him.

'He didn't do anything.' She hesitated. 'At the start.'

He clenched his jaw tight before telling her in a deathly calm tone, 'Just so we're clear. If I find out he ever laid a finger on you in anger or threatened you in any way. I'm going to find him. And I'm going to kill him.'

The smile she gave him caught the breath in his chest again. Only this time his chest twisted so painfully he could barely breathe out. So he managed a big brave old smile back at her.

'He didn't.'

'*Good.*'

'We weren't right for each other—'

'Obviously.'

She smiled again. 'If I'm going to tell you all this in one go, then you have to stop interrupting me.'

'I'm stopping, then.' He smiled at her. 'Quiet as the grave over here. Honest to God.'

The words made her laugh.

But the laugh faded, and a look of sadness crossed her eyes before she looked down at the ground and started pacing again. While Rory took a deep breath of cool air and forced himself to wait.

'I guess a part of me wanted to fit in with the rest of my family. It wasn't that I didn't feel loved; I just felt *less* than the others. Like I had something missing in me that made me a lesser person than them because I didn't giggle and chatter like they all did. I wanted to be more like them. And when Niall came along he was exactly the kind of person the twins would have dated. He was successful, his career was on the up, he was handsome and charming and they all took to him like he was some kind of long-lost relative. So, I convinced myself that he was the right man for me.'

Rory hated him even more than he already had.

'But, realistically, there were problems from early on. I just chose to ignore them.'

He could see the frown on her face as she turned round on one end of her line and headed back the other way.

'They were more my problems than his, you see.' She cleared her throat. '*Sexually speaking.* But the thing was that everything else worked so neatly—friends, family, work schedules—that it seemed like a small price to pay. To me anyway.'

How could she sell herself so short? Didn't she know she had as much right to the whole damn package as everyone else on the planet did?

Rory would never have let her settle for less. But then, by offering her a short term, no-strings attached deal, wasn't he doing exactly the same thing to her?

The thought made him scowl in annoyance.

'It was too high a price for Niall, though, given enough time to live with it. He was determined to *cure* me. It became some kind of personal goal to him. And when it didn't work he would get angry and frustrated. He would blame me, quite rightly, because it was all down to my own insecurities that I couldn't be the way he wanted me to be. So we argued.'

Her voice crackled on the last few words and Rory's heart tore for her.

She laughed a nervous, shaky laugh, and aimed a shy glance in his direction. 'You know how sarcastic I can be. Well, when we argued, I'd be a sarcastic cow and he couldn't deal with that. So he'd say things to hurt me instead. It got pretty nasty sometimes. A little scary once or twice if I'm completely honest.'

Rory was trying his absolute best not to say anything, not while the rage was building inside him at such a quick pace. There were varying forms of abuse. What she was describing wasn't physical, as he had asked her about before. No, it was a more subtle, soul-destroying method of abuse. A form of torture that had obviously affected her deeply, and played on her insecurities. If this was headed where Rory thought it was, he was still gonna have to find this guy.

When he caught sight of her lifting a hand to swipe at her cheek as she walked past him, he couldn't stop himself from interrupting again.

'He said things like what, exactly?'

The softly spoken question drew another shaky laugh from her lips. 'Oh, the usual, you know.'

Rory's reply was tight-lipped. 'Enlighten me.'

'Well, he said I was cold and unfeeling, to begin with.' Her voice wobbled again. 'During the worst arguments he used words like selfish, self-absorbed; the term frigid was a favourite.'

Rory swore viciously.

'Thing is, to a certain degree I thought he was right. I'd gotten so insular during my teens that I really believed it was a case of not being able to let someone that close. I was scared I wasn't good enough and after a while I believed it was because of the way I looked. Especially when he compared me to other women he thought were more like the way I should have been, in his eyes.' When she stopped in front of him, she swiped both hands over her cheeks and focused on a point above his head, 'I know all the things he said were in the heat of the moment and came from his own frustration. I do. And I'd pretty much accepted that that was the way I was by the end. That it couldn't be any different for me and that all I was doing was holding him back from his chance to be happier. So I let him go. I told him it wasn't his fault. And I promised myself that I'd fix the things I could fix in my life and just get on with it. Sex is a bigger thing for men than it is for women, after all.'

'Like hell it is.'

Her eyes flickered down to lock with his. 'No, really. Most women are equally happy with a half-decent chick-flick and a tub of ice cream on a Saturday night as they are with having to—'

'Lie back and think of the homeland while choosing what colour to paint the ceiling next time round?'

She smiled sadly. 'Well, pretty much.'

'And is that what you think you'd do with me, Cara?'

Rory heard her gasp. And when his gaze lowered he saw her breasts rise and fall as her breathing rate increased.

Even her answer was breathless. 'No. You're different. When I'm with you, *I'm* different.'

He'd been patient long enough. Using the palms on the wall to propel himself upward, he was in front of her in less than a second, his voice a husky grumble, 'And why do you think that is?'

Cara didn't look up at him. Instead her gaze remained focused on the V of his sweater as she answered in a low whisper. 'I have no idea.'

'How about I tell you then?' He shuffled his feet a step closer, so that his body was almost touching hers, his chin dropping towards her ear so she could hear his low voice. 'This is what they call chemistry. It's when two people have a mutual attraction for each other. There's no real scientific reason for it, not unless you want to put it down to pheromones and other emotionless hormones. But there's more to it than that with us.'

It took a long time for her head to tilt back. For her large blue eyes to lock with his again. And Rory had never in his life wanted a woman as much as he did in that instant. But it wasn't just a hormonal thing. It was a part of him, deep inside, that just simply *needed* her. To show her just what she was really capable of, with the right man.

Because there was a sensuous side to her that blew his mind. The time in the pool had had him hard as a rock all day long while he played over and over in his mind how she had reacted to the simplest of touches.

And he knew deep down in his gut, instinctively, that when they made love it was going to be amazing. For both of them. This kind of attraction didn't happen every day.

He smiled a half smile at her. 'You know that's true, don't you? You were right with me in the water today. It took as much for you to stop as it did for me.'

Cara nodded in silence.

So he reached forwards and took both of her hands in his, tangling his fingers with hers, his thumbs brushing over the beating pulses in her wrists. 'You told me that sometimes I take your breath away.'

She smiled. 'Like now, you mean?'

And he smiled back at her. 'Yes, like now. Well, like I told you, that goes both ways. I wasn't kidding when I told you that the first time you walked through the door you were the sexiest thing I'd ever seen. But what I maybe didn't mention was that the more you sparked at me, the sexier I found you. You challenged me to keep up with your wit; you put me down at every step. And no one has ever dared try that with me before.'

'Has anyone ever told you that you can be remarkably arrogant when you put your mind to it?'

He squeezed her fingers. 'You see, that's exactly what I'm talking about right there.'

She tilted her chin and smiled even more. 'So what you're saying is that you find my sarcastic put-downs a turn on?'

'Amongst other things.'

'No one has ever talked to you the way I do? *Ever?*'

'Not and got away with it.'

'You *don't* let me get away with it.'

'And that's part of the reason we spark off each other. We're equals. And that's why this is here. At least that's my take on it. Niall wasn't worthy of you. It was what was lacking in him that caused the problems. Not you. If he'd have cared the way he should have then he'd have been patient and helped you work through it. You've tried shutting me out, haven't you? And did it work? Do you see me quitting on you?'

He smiled when she shook her head, took a breath before he continued. 'No. Because I wanted you from the get-go Cara. I'd get little glimpses of the real you behind all those defences. And all it did was make me want you more.'

She tilted her head again, this time the other way, so that her mouth was angled closer to his as her eyes softened and changed colour to the shade of a summer sky before it rained. Then she flexed her fingers out, and tangled them back with his.

'So what you're saying is that the more I push you back, the more it eggs you on.'

'That's exactly what I'm saying.'

'What would happen then if I went the opposite way and made the moves on you? Did what I wanted to do without stopping to think about it? Just…did what I *wanted* to *whenever* I felt like it…'

His groin tightened at the suggestion and he smiled in the way that always seemed to get a reaction from her. 'Then I think I'd say *Thank you, God.*'

Her chin rose at the same time as a spark of confidence entered her eyes and her voice dropped.

'Don't move.'

He stood still as a rock, in more ways than one. While she

stood up onto her tiptoes and angled her mouth over his. 'Stay *absolutely* still.'

When she touched her soft mouth to his he almost groaned aloud, flexing his fingers against hers. Did that qualify as staying still and not moving? If it didn't then she had no one to blame but herself.

She had her eyes open. Staring at him as she kissed him, watching his reaction to what she was doing. It was singularly the most erotic experience of his life.

But when she ran her tongue across his lips there was just no way he could keep his eyes open any more. It was too much. So, his eyes closing, he let another groan slip free from his chest and surrendered to sensation.

He opened his mouth, angling his head to deepen the kiss, felt her nip against his bottom lip. So he moved his head forwards to meet her, allowing his mouth to slide over the soft curve of her lips, to drink in the taste of her.

And felt it as her mouth curved into a sensuous smile against his.

This woman was going to be the death of him. Every nerve in his body was straining. His heart was caught in an erratic rhythm of beating faster, then catching, then beating faster to make up the deficit. And he had no control of the feet that shuffled closer so that his lower body was pressed in against the welcoming curve of her stomach, cushioning him.

Cara giggled throatily against his mouth. 'You moved.'

He opened his eyes and stared, his mouth still on hers. 'That was involuntary. It's because I want to be inside you so bad.'

'Where I ache?'

The question was a sigh. And he groaned again in response. 'We need a room. *Now.*'

Her mouth curved again, eyes sparkling. 'There's a hotel above the restaurant.'

Rory tilted his head back and searched her eyes carefully. 'You're sure?'

Cara pursed her swollen lips in response and nodded. 'Yep.

There's always been one there. It's run by the family of the first boy I ever kissed so I'm fairly sure—'

His fingers tightened in warning. 'Right, well, we're about to make a better memory to go with that place, then. Let's go.'

She hesitated when he freed one hand and used the other to tug her along the pathway. 'What if my parents are still there?'

'I'm trained in getting into places without being seen. We'll damn well find a way.'

As they broke into a run he heard her laughing breathlessly at his side. 'I thought we were going to wait until we couldn't stand it any more?'

Rory stopped abruptly, allowing her to get one running step in front of him before he tugged hard on her hand, and hauled her against him for another white-hot kiss. Then he lifted his head and grumbled, 'Honey, I'm already there.'

CHAPTER THIRTEEN

CARA WAS BREATHLESS by the time they reached the room.

And not just from the fact they'd pretty much run, hand in hand, the whole way back to the hotel. There was also the fun and games involved with checking her parents weren't still in the restaurant bar, the embarrassment of checking into the hotel with Mr Harrigan, father of the boy she had shared her first teenage kiss with, and the two-steps-at-a-time rush up the narrow stairs to the room.

She had giggled like a schoolgirl the whole way there.

But inside the room, in the dark, with her back pressed against the door and Rory's silhouette in front of her, she just simply *couldn't* breathe any more. No matter how the almost painful beating of her heart demanded it.

Because she had waited her whole life to be with someone like Rory, hadn't she?

It felt as if every second of her existence had been leading her to this moment, in this room, with this man.

It was like riding along on a tidal wave of anticipation. It was the expectation of what was to come.

She wanted him so much that there wasn't room for doubt. There was just the aching, the heat. And the deep-seated need to have him buried deeply inside her, filling her.

But it was the sound of him, equally as breathless as she was, that stole her heart from her. Where had he been when she'd been so lost and so alone before?

He didn't speak.

There was no sound in the darkened room apart from their breathing and the distant sounds of harbour traffic. Until there was the soft sound of wool shifting over skin as he lifted his arms and pulled his sweater over his head.

Then he was closer to her, his hands reaching for hers as his ragged breath fanned over her face.

'*Cara.*'

Her name had never sounded so sensual. Cara. Friend, it meant, in the ancient Irish. And Cara had never before felt the meaning of it so deeply. She *felt* like a friend to him and that he was hers in return. But more than that: she felt she was his equal, his soon-to-be-lover. And on her own terms, with her taking the lead and living out her fantasies if she chose to.

The most potent of combinations.

He pulled their joined hands upwards, pressed them against the door above her head. And then his mouth was on her damp skin, his lips blazing a trail along the arch of her neck as her head dropped back. Lower still, tracing the edge of her frilled linen blouse to the curve of her breast at the sweetheart neckline.

Cara arched her spine from the door in response, heard her own breathy sigh.

'*Yes.*'

He kept her hands trapped above her head, this time in one of his. Tracing the fingertips of his free hand along the arch of one of her upwardly stretched arms, from wrist to elbow, from elbow to the inward curve where her arm met her shoulder, causing her to squirm at the ticklish sensation, then along the side of her breast and over the aching mound to the buttons that would free her.

His head rose, mouth fastening on hers, feeding hungrily as he eased each ivory button from its slot until her blouse was open. Then his head rose again, dipping down to the curve of soft skin above the lace of her bra.

The redundant fingertips skimmed over the material on the

breast he wasn't ministering with soft kisses; they circled, felt the weight, skimmed over her nipple until it throbbed against the lace.

And Cara moaned throatily in response.

'Slowly, honey,' he mumbled against her breast. 'Slowly works best, trust me. No matter what we might both think right this minute.'

His head lifted, mouth hovering over hers as she whimpered in protest. '*S-l-o-w-l-y.*'

Cara didn't want slowly. She wanted fast and hard. She wanted the kind of completion she'd never felt before. Her whole body was straining towards it, burning, every nerve end sensitized to an almost painful level.

So that when his fingertips moved from her straining nipple and around her back to the catch on her bra she almost cried out again.

It was undone with one flick of his wrist.

Goose-pimples immediately appeared on her flesh as cool air hit heated skin. It was torture.

'Uh-h,' She was eloquent in the throes of wanton passion, apparently.

Rory tore his mouth from hers and husky laughter reached her ears before he moved his fingertips back round to push the material upwards. Then his hot mouth was there, replacing the scratch of the lace with the velvet of his tongue.

Cara's knees gave out.

But the hard length of his body pressed in to hold her in place while he continued to torture her until she was writhing and moaning like some kind of wanton hussy.

'Rory!'

His head lifted at the sound of his name, forced out on a tortured whisper. 'Yes?'

'*Please!*'

He smiled in the darkness. 'Please what?'

Cara swore softly, then, 'You know what!'

'Well, I'm pretty sure we just paid for a bed.'

Cara struggled to get her hands free, placing them against the hard wall of his naked chest, pushing him back. 'Then let's use it shall we?'

'Works for me.' He laughed again. 'We might just need to remember this position for future reference though.'

She fastened her mouth to his smiling one as they staggered backwards. Bodies spinning round, once, twice.

Their mouths parted, and they laughed in unison.

'Well, this is romantic. I don't think I've ever had a woman laugh this much before. I should really take offence.'

Cara continued laughing—a low, husky, purely sexual laugh—while Rory stepped back a little and freed his hands to slide the material he had loosened down her arms.

'At least I'll be memorable.'

The dark shadow of his face loomed over her, his voice a low grumble. 'I won't forget you.'

They were the sweetest words she had ever heard. Because she had heard empty endearments before, had listened to promises being made that had never been meant to be kept.

She didn't need him to tell her he cared. She already knew. It was there in the husky timbre of his deep voice, was there in the hands that shook as he reached for her naked breasts and covered them. It was there in his ragged breathing. And when she lifted her hand and placed it on his chest, it was there in the pounding of his heart.

'Neither will I.'

His kiss sealed the promise. While his fingers kneaded her breasts, found her distended nipples and teased them until she thought she'd spontaneously combust from just that touch. She could have stood there and had him do just that for hours, but the knot of tension in her abdomen was growing, tightening, the muscles bunching in preparation for the filling of her body with his.

Their tongues met, tangled, his teeth caught her lower lip and tugged.

Then his hands moved, drawing a low moan of displeasure from her before he smoothed around her body and wrapped her in his arms, drawing her tight against his chest. Skin to skin; sensitized breasts against chest hair.

One hand snaked up her back and tangled in her hair, tugged gently as his mouth lifted and the tilt of her head gave him access to her neck.

Wet lips blazed over her hot skin, his tongue dipping into the hollow of her collar-bone. He nipped her shoulder.

And Cara's heavy head sank back against his tangled fingers as she made low murmurs of pleasure and encouragement, sighing deeply, gasping. Each small sound growing progressively louder in the silence of the room as he continued.

He kissed small, warm, wet kisses over each breast, worked back up to her collar-bone to dip his tongue again.

'I want to touch you.'

Her hands were already roving over his back, following the line from his tapered waist to his broad shoulders, where she grasped hold of the bunched muscles. But it wasn't enough. Not nearly enough.

Rory's head shook against her neck. 'Not yet.'

He kissed along her neck, along her jaw, angling her head with his hand so she was open to him. 'If you touch me anywhere else, then I'm going to have real problems with the going slow.'

Cara opened her mouth to argue, but he silenced her with his. Moving her to the edge of the bed, his hands shifted again, this time under her arms to lift her onto the soft surface. The mattress dipped, rolling them towards each other.

Caressing one breast, he drew the nipple of the other into the heated cavern of his mouth. Cara writhed against him in response and he lifted his head, rubbing his chin back and forth over the breast he had just suckled, rough against smooth.

'Hell, woman, how did you ever let yourself think you weren't a highly sexual being?'

'I hadn't met you before.'

It was the right answer for him. And Rory felt his mouth curve into a satisfied smile. Everything about her was sexual, the way she was twisting her lush body beside him, the small noises she would make when he kissed her breasts or tasted her skin. The protests she would make when he slowed down, or moved away from where she was getting the most pleasure.

She was every man's dream. Every response feeding his ego and urging him to give more so that her release would be so fierce he would have no choice but to follow her over the edge.

Rory turned onto his side, tracing a line down her body, from her collar-bone, over her breast, down over each rib to the curve of her stomach. The temptation to reach for a light switch was so strong it almost ate him up. But this first time he could make some concessions. It would be easier for Cara in the dim light, would magnify what she could feel in the absence of her sight. And the shadows he could see only made it all more sensual than it already was for him.

He hadn't lied when he had told her he wouldn't forget. He didn't want to forget. He wanted to remember every curve of her body, how soft her skin felt to the touch, her sweet scent. He wanted to paint a picture of her in his mind like a blind man memorizing a face for the first time: by touch alone. But most of all he wanted the memory of her falling apart in his arms.

So he traced his hand lower, feeling for the edge of her bunched skirt. When he found it and began to draw it upwards, his forefinger on the softer skin of her inner thigh, she tried to turn tighter towards him, her hands reaching out frantically for him.

'Don't move, honey. Close your eyes and feel. Let me do all the work this first time.'

His forefinger reached the edge of her panties, felt lace, traced the edge until he found the top and her abdomen flexed beneath his touch. Then he bunched the material of the skirt on her stomach and slipped his fingers under the band. 'Lift your hips.'

She lifted, her legs parting a little as he drew the lace down. Whispering it over her thighs slowly, so slowly, until her knees rose and she lifted her feet for him.

When he traced his forefinger back up he felt her tense, heard the sound of her head twisting back and forth on the covers. So he moved up a little on the bed and searched for her mouth, his tongue seeking access at the same time as his long finger.

Cara moaned into his mouth.

His finger traced through the slick warmth, circled the moisture around until his thumb smoothed over her clitoris and her hips bucked upwards in response.

She tore her mouth free to gasp his name.

'Shh.' He nuzzled in the hair next to her ear, 'Take a deep breath.'

Her breasts rose and fell beside his chest as she took a ragged breath.

'Good girl. That's it.' His finger circled, moved back to her most sensitive place again as he whispered, 'Slowly.'

'*I can't—*'

'Yes, you can. You just need to control it.' He circled again, then back, creating a velvet covering below his fingertips. 'Are your eyes closed?'

'Yes.' She breathed out the word, her neck arching beside his chin. 'Damn you. Yes.'

Her hips bucked up against his hand again.

'Can you feel it, Cara? Can you feel yourself on the edge? You just have to let yourself fall, that's all. Let go.' He kissed the soft skin behind her ear and whispered again, 'Come for me. And I'll catch you when you fall.'

Her whole body was twisting beside him, one of her hands gripping onto his shoulders, fingernails digging into his skin.

He kissed her skin again, his whispered voice muffled. 'I've got you.'

He slipped two fingers along and inside, then increased the pressure on her clitoris with his thumb.

Cara sucked in air. She went still.

Her body spasmed around his fingers; her neck strained as she pushed her head deeper into the covers. And then she cried out, long and low, and jerked against his hand, again and again.

Rory smiled against her ear while he listened to her breathing slow from long, shuddering breaths to deeper ones while she made small murmurs of satisfaction and the tight hold on his fingers relaxed.

Then he heard her breath shake.

He felt her throat spasm against his nose as she swallowed. And her breath shook again.

When he lifted his hand from her and raised his knuckle to her face he could feel the moisture there and his heart tore in two. Had he hurt her? Was that what she had been trying to tell him all along: that it caused her physical pain? And he hadn't been listening?

Please, he sent a silent plea upwards; *don't let me have hurt her.*

He raised his head to try and see her in the dim light. But she buried her face in against his neck and sobbed.

'Cara?'

'I'm fine.' She laughed nervously, half laugh, half sob, her voice a shaky whisper muffled by his skin. 'I'm better than fine.'

'Did I hurt you?'

Her hand curled up, found his jaw and she came out of her hiding place to kiss him, salt from her tears on her lips. 'No, but you may have killed me a little.'

He chuckled against her mouth, drawing her into his arms and squeezing her closer as he breathed out with relief. 'I told you slow was better.'

'Well, it certainly worked for me.' Her mouth curved against his. 'Now we just have to see what works for you.'

Her lips moved over his in a gentle kiss while her hands began a tentative exploration of his chest. And Rory leaned onto his back, more than willing to let her make whatever exploration she felt like making.

Truth be told, in his current state, it wasn't going to take much. While she had been drawing his fingers deep inside in the throes of her orgasm he had been twitching, desperate to be where his fingers were.

He curled an arm up over her head and toyed with the soft ends of her hair, the scent of her shampoo surrounding him. Met her halfway when she deepened the kiss, darted the end of her tongue along his lips to seek entry. Then she leaned back and nipped his bottom lip, dragging it back a little before she released him.

Her foot was stroking up and down his calf. 'How come I'm wearing less than you are?'

'Because I'm a smooth operator?'

'What happened to us being equals?'

He continued toying with the ends of her hair. 'We are equals. You're more than a match for me and you know it. You just showed me how much of a match. In fact, you just may be the death of me if you come like that again when I'm inside you.'

Her head tilted towards his throat, loose strands of hair tickling against his cheek. And Rory sensed the moment of hesitation before she spoke.

'When do you go back?'

They both knew she didn't mean the gym.

Rory lifted his free hand from her waist and enfolded one of hers where it lay against his chest. He squeezed, just the one time. 'A couple of weeks.'

He waited, a part of him almost willing her to ask him about their arrangement to disappear out of each other's lives. Which shocked him. Not so much in that he wanted her to ask, but that a part of him almost needed her to.

He'd never needed it before, had never wanted to have someone waiting for him to come home. Because he'd never felt that he could make even that small a commitment to someone else. Long-distance relationships didn't work, not unless they were the no-strings-attached purely sex variety, which he would never ask of her. No, with Cara it would be more than that. And he had seen some of the other guys he worked with try, and unless they were married and therefore felt they had no choice but to try, it rarely worked. Even being married was no guarantee.

He couldn't put either of them through a mess like that and Cara didn't need another disastrous relationship.

But a part of him still ached at the thought of leaving her behind.

What did *she* want?

Her other hand, the one that had been toying almost absent-mindedly with his chest hair, moved lower and she ran her nails along the skin at the top of his jeans.

His muscles jerked.

'We can do a lot in two weeks.'

Rory swallowed hard. 'I'm open to suggestions.'

'I believe that.'

He breathed out, surprised to find he had been holding his breath. Then sucked it back in as her hand traced his erection where it was pressing painfully against the crotch of his jeans.

'You don't really want to be wearing more than me, do you? It seems an awful waste.'

She was already pulling her hand from his on his chest, both hands freeing the buttons on his jeans. Each 'pop' making him strain against her knuckles.

'I've created a monster, haven't I?'

'Well, I'm all for equality.' She ran her fingernails along his hard shaft. 'I might need some help getting these jeans off, though. And you better tell me you have something with you or your reputation is going to take a tumble.'

She grazed him again and he groaned. 'Back pocket. Wallet. And that skirt needs to go, too. I don't want anything getting in the way.'

There were a few moments of ungracious scrambling as they fumbled with clothes and his wallet. And then Cara's hand wrapped around his, folding the foil wrapper into his palm as her mouth hovered over his. 'You said you wouldn't forget this.'

'And I meant it.'

She opened his fist and took the wrapper from him. 'I want you to remember. For the next two weeks—' there was the sound of foil being torn '—I want us to make enough memories to last a lifetime.'

The part of him that had ached before at the thought of leaving her broke apart inside him. 'We can do that.'

Her hands moved down, one feeling along his thigh for his

scar. Her fingertips circled it, smoothed over the wrinkled skin and traced the indentation. 'Just promise me that if something ever happened to you again that someone would tell me. That's all I ask, Rory. I don't want to spend my life wondering.'

He wouldn't want her to.

She brought her hand up, wrapped her fingers around him and stroked his hard length. And Rory couldn't think for a minute; couldn't concentrate on anything beyond her soft hand on him, coiling around, stroking up and then down.

He rolled towards her, his voice a low rumble. 'Where's the condom?'

'I'm doing it.'

'Not fast enough, hon.' He prized it from her fingers and kissed her long and hard.

He had meant to take his time with her again, but the newly empowered Cara had other ideas. While he fumbled with shaking hands she rolled his way, swung her leg over his and straddled him, her hands pressing down on his chest.

When she kissed him, full on and open mouthed, her hair fell forward, surrounding his face, creating a scented cocoon that sent sparks of brightly coloured light across the backs of his eyelids.

Hips poised above him, she whispered against his mouth, 'Promise me.'

Rory wanted to tell her that nothing would happen. That he'd be fine and she wouldn't have to worry. But he couldn't guarantee that, could he?

Any more than he could make a promise to make their relationship work beyond what they already had.

She slid downwards, taking him in inch by torturous inch. 'Promise me.'

'I promise.'

She sank fully onto him, held him deep inside, and then arched back and moaned.

There wasn't any more conversation after that. There was

just a slow build as she undulated her hips on him, and the sounds of their ragged breathing.

'*Cara.*' He could feel his body straining for release, his heart pounding painfully in his chest.

But she didn't answer. And he could feel her tightening around him, drawing him deeper inside. So he reached down, sought and found the little nerve that would bring her with him.

Cara let out a small cry of surprise, stilled again.

How could she think he would ever forget this?

Because Rory knew in his soul as he called out her name again that he never would. Not ever.

CHAPTER FOURTEEN

'WHAT ARE YOU doing?'

Rory glanced over at his brother as he walked round the counter, then looked back to see Cara smile at him as she left. He smiled in return, his heart warming, then focused fully on Connor.

'I said I'd get the paperwork done.'

'I'm not talking about the paperwork.'

'Then I have no idea what you mean.' Which wasn't entirely true. He had caught Connor looking at him with Cara more than enough the last few days.

It had to be pretty obvious to the outside world anyway. Because Rory couldn't remember the last time he had laughed so much, the last time he had felt a need to reach out for a woman as much as he did with Cara. She was under his skin. His first thought in the morning and last thing at night; when her body was wrapped around his.

And he'd barely set foot in his brother's house since the night they'd spent in the hotel.

There were bound to be questions somewhere along the way.

'You know our policy on hitting on clients.'

'Cara's different.'

'Is she indeed?' Connor turned round and leaned back against the counter, his arms folded across his chest. 'Well, maybe you should just talk me through that one.'

'I would if I thought it was any of your business.'

'She seems nice.'

She was way more than nice. And Rory felt his mouth curve again at the thought of the many things she was. Adventurous was certainly high on the list now.

Connor shook his head. 'You're not actually going to tell me you feel something for her?'

'And what the hell does that mean?'

'Not exactly your usual type, is she?'

Rory's back straightened. *'Meaning?'*

There was a small smile on Connor's face, one laced with bitterness. 'Meaning she's the kind of woman men get seriously involved with. And you're not the kind of guy who does that. And she's a *client*. You can't go breaking hearts on your own front doorstep and then leave me with the mess after you've gone.'

Even though what he was saying made a small modicum of sense, Rory felt his anger rise. Connor had always been sensible enough not to get involved in his elder brother's affairs. And it wasn't as if he could throw stones in the broken hearts department.

'Butt out, Connor.'

But Connor didn't take the hint. Even when Rory walked back round the counter and headed down the hall to the changing rooms,

'So what, then? You gonna go all pipe and slippers after twelve years and get a nine to five? *C'mon!* We both know that's not going to happen. So where does that leave her, Rory? Dangling on a thread waiting for you to come home and work out all that sexual frustration on your next trip home? Now that's romantic.'

'You're walking a thin line.'

'If you care about her, then you won't do that to her.'

Rory pushed the changing-room door so hard it bounced off the door stop and slammed closed again. He turned, fixing his brother with a warning glare. 'You don't have any idea how I feel about her!'

'Do you?'

He stopped. His hands clenched into fists at his sides, jaw clenching. Discussing how he felt about Cara wasn't something he was about to do with his kid brother. Especially when he wasn't really sure how he felt himself.

How did he explain to someone else how it felt when she fell asleep in his arms? Or when she would smile in the morning before she even opened her eyes? How it felt to have her laugh out loud at something cocky he said or come out with something so quick-witted that he was still laughing even after he left her?

Connor took a step closer. 'I've seen how you look at her, Rory. And you're one step away from asking her to wait for you, aren't you?'

Rory took a moment to swallow down his anger at Connor's interference. He looked past him, took a breath, and then looked him square in the eye. 'That would hardly be fair on her, now, would it?'

'You're damn right it wouldn't be!' All the reply seemed to have done was rouse Connor further. He pointed an angry finger at his brother's chest. 'There are enough women who care about you already living every day in fear. You can't go doing that to another one.'

'What in hell are you talking about now?'

Connor nodded. 'You know what I'm talking about.'

When he turned on his heel and stalked back down the hallway, Rory was hot on his heels. He wasn't letting this one go. 'Don't go chicken on me now, Connor. You've got something you want to say, then you spit it out.'

Connor kept walking.

So Rory scanned the hall for a place to get them away from their clients' prying eyes. He'd been in enough bust-ups with his brothers over the years to know when another one was approaching.

A storage cupboard caught his eye. That should do.

When they were close he wrapped the crook of his arm around Connor's neck and wrestled him into it. Towels and spare pieces of light equipment hit the floor as Connor fought himself free. And then they faced off, both of them glaring angrily.

Rory blocked the door and folded his arms across his chest. 'Spit it out.'

'*Fine.* You want it, then you've got it. And it's been a bloody long time coming!' He stepped forwards and poked his brother hard in the chest. 'You're a selfish bastard, Rory. You think that every time you go back over there that I don't have to watch every female in our family break their heart? It was fear of the unknown before. They'd worry about what *might* happen without knowing what *could* happen. Until you went all commando on us and bloody well almost got yourself killed! And now you're all healed up you're going straight back there and I get to deal with what's left behind. Like always.'

Rory frowned as Connor paused for breath, the emotion in his eyes saying as much as his angry words. 'Well, you needn't think I'm taking on another one just so you can go play the action hero.'

'If I wasn't bloody well playing the action hero, then we wouldn't have this place! Or the other two. And where would we all be then, Connor? You tell me.'

Connor laughed in his face. 'Oh, that might have worked a few years ago. But we both know it's steady enough here now for you to quit trying to support every damn one of us by putting your neck on the line.'

Rory didn't answer him.

And Connor nodded, lifting a hand to run it back through his hair as he took another breath. Then he looked back at his brother. 'You're not doing this for the family any more, Rory. You're doing it for the people over there. I get that. That's what you do; you take responsibility for the whole bloody world. Thing is at some point you're either going to get yourself killed or you're going to realize that every one of those guys will eventually move on and make lives of their own. And what the hell have you got then? Another country, another set of people you don't know that you'll automatically lay your life on the line for? When is it enough? How much do you have to give?'

'I'll know when it's time to quit, Connor. I'm not suicidal.' Rory searched for the words to try and make his brother understand. 'You don't know what it's like. If you did then you'd know why I keep going back.'

'You're right, I don't know. But I know you.' He seemed to back down a little. 'You're *my brother.* And I don't want to stand over a hole in the ground any more than Mum does.'

'I can't leave those guys out there without me.'

'Then don't make that woman stand and wait for you like everyone else does; waiting for that phone call to come. Not if you care about her. There's enough of us doing that already.'

'I haven't asked her to.'

'Maybe not, but can you honestly tell me that if she wanted to you'd stop her?' He reached his hands out and rested them on Rory's shoulders. 'She's as nuts about you as you are on her. It's written all over the two of you. And don't think I don't know what a big thing that is for you, 'cos I do. She must be some amazing woman for you to feel like that.'

'She is.'

Connor nodded again. 'Well, if she is then she's worth staying for. I could do with you here. The business could expand again. The family could sleep at night again and stop dying a little every time they see a news report from where you are. You just need to decide whether you're going to hold on to her or whether you're going to let her go. 'Cos there isn't a half measure here for you; not if you love her that much and want her to be happy.'

Cara was sick of fighting with herself.

It was a bit pointless fighting the truth, after all. She had fought it for years with Niall and look where that had got her! It had taken a man like Rory Flanaghan in her life for her to see what she was capable of feeling.

And the truth was she was in love.

Now that she had worked her way through so many other things, she was finally able to say she knew what her strengths and weaknesses were. She knew she had wasted years of her life over stupid paranoia and self-doubt, instead of focusing on the positive things.

Being head over heels in love for the first time was a big positive. The fact that she knew she was going to have her heart broken *wasn't*.

But she wanted her two weeks of memories. She needed them. Because, having denied herself a real sense of happiness for so long, she had to reach out and grab it while it was there. Even when each day brought her closer to her deadline with him and the heartache that would come with it.

Even when every day it was getting tougher to hide the truth from him and not show him how she was dying a little inside.

The night before, when he had spent hours exploring her body and winding her so tight she had practically wept from the sheer pleasure of it, she had almost told him. She had almost said she would wait for him, for as long as he wanted her to.

But he hadn't asked her, hadn't even hinted at it. The arrangement had been clear from the start. He wasn't the kind of man to stay in one place for long. Wasn't the 'stay at home type' as he had once so clearly stated. And for all the joy she knew she would get from seeing him when he did come home, she also doubted she was strong enough to see him come home in pieces as his friend had.

Or, worse, not come home at all.

No. She would take the brief happiness while it was there. And then she would move on and make the other changes she had planned from the start. She'd build a whole new life to go with the new Cara that being with Rory had helped her see in herself.

She would show him how much she loved him by being everything she could be. By taking chances and making adventures. By grabbing life by the throat and not restricting herself to a tiny corner of the universe.

Despite the fact they would soon go back to leading the very different lives they had before, having the confidence to do the things she'd only dreamed of doing was exhilarating. Her life had changed. She had changed.

Even though she was going to have to let go of the most important man in her life, she wasn't going to let herself curl up in a ball and wither away. No more hiding from life—the bad or the good.

And she was smiling at that massive achievement when he appeared at her door. 'I have life insurance, thanks.'

'You're a very funny woman.' He smiled at her and pushed his shoulder off the wall. 'Anyone ever tell you that?'

Cara leaned up for her kiss, smiling against his mouth. 'Is that funny ha-ha or funny peculiar?'

'The jury's still out.'

She kissed him again, then stood back a little to point a finger at him as she retreated. 'You're early.'

'I needed some space from my brother.'

Cara's eyes widened in surprise. 'You had a row? Does that happen often? I thought you said you two were close?'

And he had, she remembered distinctly every word of every conversation they'd had when lying together in bed after making love. They were all part of the memories store now, tucked safely away in her heart.

Rory closed the door behind him and glanced briefly at her face before he made his way to the huge overstuffed sofa. 'We are. He was giving me some home truths about the family's feelings about my going back to work.'

Cara watched as he flopped down onto the sofa, her eyes only leaving him long enough for her to hit the save key on her laptop before she walked round to him. 'I take it they're worried?'

She knew how that went. And she felt closer to the unknown members of his family for it. As if in some way she had the right to feel as if she was one of them because she loved him, too.

'They always worry. But it's a bit harder this time.'

She took the hand he held up for her when she was closer, settling herself beside him and swinging her legs over his lap. 'That'll have something to do with the whole being shot thing.'

Rory's large hand toyed with her fingers while his other hand rubbed up and down her thigh, his eyes focused on a worn patch on her jeans. 'I'd say so. Connor thinks I'm selfish for going back and making them worry again. He'd like me to stay here and run the business with him.'

A part of Cara wished he were the kind of man who could do that. But she knew him better. 'It would kill you knowing all your friends were over there without you.'

He flashed a smile at her. 'That's what I told him.'

'They're your family. They just want you somewhere safe, is all. But they wouldn't want you unhappy, either. So they'll have to accept that loving you means they have to let you do what you need to do.'

'If I gave you a number could you call and say that over the phone?'

Cara laughed. 'If I thought it would make a difference I would try for you.'

'My hero.'

She noticed how the smile in his eyes faded before he looked down at her legs again. The argument with his brother had obviously affected him deeply. But it was tough for her not to empathize with Connor's point of view. Just because she had come to terms with Rory leaving didn't mean others could do the same. Not that she was dealing particularly well with it herself.

She studied his profile for a long while, watched his thick lashes flicker as he followed the movement of his hand on her thigh, and she smiled softly as the familiar warmth built inside her body for him. After all the tension there had been between them before they had made love, it still amazed her that wanting him wasn't any the less for them having completed the act. *Lots*.

Just looking at him was enough to start the knot in her abdomen forming. Even more so now that she knew what he could do to her. She doubted she would ever tire of him that way.

But he hadn't tired any, either. They were still equal on that score.

She reached a hand up and played with the coarse hair at the nape of his neck. 'It's the first time you've got really hurt, though, isn't it?'

Rory grimaced slightly.

And Cara's eyes widened again. '*Isn't it?*'

'That I've told them about.'

Her hand stilled.

So he turned his face towards her, a small smile on his mouth. 'Do you tell your family every time *you* get in trouble? Knowing all the associated worry and well-meaning lectures that would go with it?'

'Have you been shot before?'

'Shot *at.*'

'How many times?'

He shrugged. 'A few.'

She tilted her head and blinked at him.

And he chuckled. 'Honey, I might have to get you to sign a piece of paper before I tell you much more. I've never talked to anyone that wasn't on the job about this stuff. It's not something I'm used to—all this sharing.'

She smiled at the confession, 'That goes both ways, big guy.' A breath. 'Well, you'd better not mention it to your family unless you want another row with Connor about it.'

He examined her face for a long time. 'How come you're fine with it?'

'Oh, I'm not fine with it. It's just a little surreal to me. All I know is here and now.' She cradled the back of his head in her hand and smiled softly across at him. 'You being here where I can touch you and see you is my reality. That's all I need.'

Rory stared at her for a long, long while, with such an intense expression on his face that Cara's smile almost faded. But just when she thought she'd given herself away a low sound erupted from his lips, half groan, half sigh, and he jerked his head.

'Come over here.'

Squashing a little closer, she lifted her arms and circled them around the strong column of his neck, pulling her upper body tight against his chest as he buried his face in her hair.

'I missed you.'

She laughed above his head. 'You saw me less then three hours ago, remember? You made me do twice the length of a workout I normally do.'

'That was ages ago.'

'You're right.' She felt him pushing her back down on the sofa and she let him, smiling as he moved his hand under the edge of her thigh and cupped her rear. 'It *was* ages ago. And for the record, I missed you, too.'

His head rose, face hovering above hers, dark eyes sparkling dangerously. 'Have I mentioned that those pelvic lifts you do make me insane?'

'A time or two.'

'And you do them slower on purpose don't you, madam?'

She made an exaggerated nod. 'Yes, I do. I happen to like making you insane.'

'Well, you know what they say.'

'And what do they say?'

'Turnabout—' he brushed his mouth over hers '—is fair—' and again, a deeper kiss this time that sent her blood rushing faster through her veins '—play.'

He ran his hand up her back as he continued to assault her senses with his mouth. When he found her arm he searched towards her wrist, finally stretching their joined hands up over her head.

And knocked a lamp off the side table.

They both turned and looked at it on the ground.

Then Rory noticed what else they had knocked over. 'Plane tickets?' He looked back into her eyes. 'Going somewhere?'

Cara's breath caught in her chest. But she covered it with a smile. 'I was always going somewhere. It was part of the make-changes-in-my-life plan from the start. But the tickets only came today.'

Rory frowned down at her. 'When are you going?'

'Three weeks from now. Straight after Laura's wedding.'

'Where to?'

'On a grand adventure. I've spent too long living here with my whole world in such a tiny space. The all-new, improved Cara Sheehan wants to see the world.'

It was taking everything she had to keep the bright note in her voice. Praying that he didn't see behind it to her reasons for not wanting to be there for a while when he had gone. She'd always wanted to make the trip. This had just brought it forward, was all.

Staying there, surrounded by all the places they had been, with all the associated memories, would just be too much. But he didn't need to know that part.

'How long will you be away?'

'At least three months.'

He continued to frown.

And Cara panicked. She couldn't give him time to figure it out. Couldn't have him looking at her with anything resembling regret, or chance him trying to make an apology for anything they had done, or the fact she had given him her heart when he had never asked for it.

'Now that I can actually wear a bikini you wouldn't want the world to miss out on seeing me in it, would you?'

'Just so long as looking is all the world does.'

The possessive edge to his voice tore her chest in two. Oh, no, he couldn't go all 'you're my woman' on her. If he did that then she might make the mistake of telling him she was. So she framed one side of his face with a hand and forced a light tone to her voice as she kissed him.

'I'm going to live a little. Without any more hang-ups, thanks to a little help from you. For the first time, I'm going to go out there and see what life has for me beyond these four walls now that I finally have the confidence to go see. You should be pretty damn proud of your help in that transformation.'

Rory lifted her hand off his face. 'Oh, that's sweet, *thanks.*' He sat up and removed her legs from his lap. 'You're off to play with all your new found *skills* and I'm supposed to be *pleased* about that?'

'Now wait just a *damn minute—*'

CHAPTER FIFTEEN

RORY PUSHED UP onto his feet, a cruel smile on his face. What had Cara expected, after all?

He hadn't planned to walk straight in and tell her about the argument he'd had with Connor. And yet, talking to her about it was the first thing he had done. As if her reaction to the subject matter was so vital for him to know that he hadn't been able to stop himself.

And she'd been great about it. Better than great. She had understood how he felt, had accepted him as the kind of man he was—which was more than he could ever have hoped for.

It had given him hope that they might find a way to make things work.

When she had said that his being there was all the reality she needed, he had been the closest to telling her that he had ever been; even closer than the times when he was buried deep within her body and she was flexing around him as she fell over the edge. When his name would be on her lips and he just wanted to hold her closer and tell her how much she meant to him.

Connor had been right.

If she had said she would wait for him then he would have wanted her to. Because he knew in his soul that coming home each time would mean more than it had before, because he would be coming home to Cara.

To find out she had already planned to not be there, to be away off somewhere on *adventures*. Well, how the bloody hell did she *expect* him to react to that?

It just bugged the hell out of him that she had been able to stick to the rules better than he had.

'No, I get it. That was the deal anyway, wasn't it? No strings. Well, good for you. I guess this means you don't need that refund.' He added a wink for good measure. 'Told you I was the best, didn't I?'

She looked as if he had just slapped her.

And he felt a wave of guilt cross his chest for hurting her. But if he told her the real reason he was angry, it would be even messier than it already was, right? And he'd look like a pathetic idiot—which wasn't a look that suited him.

So he just shook his head and walked round the bottom end of the sofa.

'Where do you think you're going?'

Cara surprised him by how quickly she got up and made it to the front door, barring his way with her hands on her hips and an angry glare. 'You can't just say something like that and then storm off in a strop!'

'Well, stupid me for being mad that you're off round the world looking to put all your new-found experience to good use!'

'I didn't say that!' She looked completely flabbergasted by the suggestion, her eyes wide and flashing in annoyance. 'You *moron!* Taking this trip was planned before I even met you and it has nothing to do with going on a quest for men and everything to do with seeing places I've wanted to see my entire life!'

She stepped closer, shaking her head. 'You just don't get it, do you? *Look around you!'*

When she lifted an arm and waved it out to one side, his eyes followed the movement, scanning over the large, somewhat chaotic room. He had teased her about it when they'd first tumbled through her front door on the way to her bedroom. But he had liked it.

Shelves crammed to overflowing with books of different

shapes and sizes, big, comfortably worn chairs, way more furniture than she probably needed. It was a home. And Rory had liked that. It had been a very small part of the reason he had practically lived there for over a week.

His gaze came back to her flushed face as she continued. 'This has been my universe since I left my parents' house. Or at the very least the centre of it. And I've never gone anywhere that wasn't less than half a day's drive away. I'm practically a bloody hermit!'

Rory frowned a little at the revelation.

While Cara laughed, he stood still and listened. The slight tremor in her voice was audible to his well-trained ears as she continued. 'You were right when you said that I didn't just join the gym to drop a few pounds. I was there to make changes. It was the first step, is all.'

She laughed again. 'I write books for a living, for crying out loud. You think that's a sociable kind of a job? And the irony is that, behind the humour in them, they're basically self-help books. Like all along I was trying to tell myself something and just wasn't listening.'

Her blue eyes searched his impassive face for a long moment before she sighed, her arm rising again and dropping to her side in resignation. 'When Niall left I guess I knew it was time to practise more of what I preached. Because what I was doing wasn't living; it was *existing*, filling in time. And that needed to change if I was ever going to stand a chance of being happy.'

He watched the differing emotions as they passed over her face. And knew it wasn't just a case of him being able to read them better because he had spent time with her.

She *had* changed.

When he had met her she'd hidden behind sarcasm, guarded what she thought and felt as if it was too dangerous a thing to be open. It had been why she'd fought him so hard, hadn't it?

Maybe a part of him had even known that from the beginning and that was why he had pushed so hard?

She frowned, looked downwards, then up, shifting from one

foot to another. Not looking him in the eye. It was almost a glimpse of how she had been at the start, minus the sarcastic quips and put-downs.

Then she took a breath, tilted her head back and confessed, 'Never once in the great plan to change my life did I think there would be a *you*.'

Her chin tilted down again and Rory's heart caught at the sight of a shimmer in her eyes. He didn't want her to cry. She shouldn't ever have to cry any more. Not when she'd come so far in such a short time. And certainly not because he'd just been such a complete ass.

He couldn't be responsible for her tears.

'Cara—'

'No, wait.' She held a hand up in front of her body. 'I need to tell you this. Because I care about you enough to want you to know it all.'

It wasn't that he didn't know she cared. He did. It was probably why the argument with Connor had had such an impact. Because the things he had said had all been founded on what was the truth. And Rory had known she cared for a while now. It wasn't as if he were some naive kid, after all. He'd known because he felt the same way. And when something just felt so *right,* there hadn't seemed any point in analyzing it or trying to seek confirmation of it.

But maybe the reason he hadn't was because he had known how delicate it was, how easily shattered.

Standing in front of her now, looking at her with her flushed cheeks and her shimmering eyes, Rory knew it wasn't enough. If he had his way, she would more than *care.*

She would feel it as soul-deep as he did.

When he didn't speak she took another breath, her hand lowering back to her side.

'I knew what I was getting into with you, Rory. Maybe not right at the start. But I knew there was a time limit. We both did. And I want you to know that I wouldn't go back and change any of it. So I don't want you to leave feeling guilty about anything or thinking that I expect you to come back to me. Or that I'm taking this trip to run away because of you.'

She looked away for a moment.

So Rory studied her profile for a long while, memorizing her as if he had just seen her for the first time when she was already indelibly imprinted on his mind and in his heart. He didn't just know that her deep brown hair had coppery tints when the sun shone on it; he knew how it felt between his fingertips and surrounding his face, knew how its soft scent would for evermore remind him of her. He knew how her large blue eyes could sparkle with amusement as a precursor of a quick witticism, or shadow with a doubt, or darken with desire when she wanted him. How her mouth would slowly curve into a smile when he teased her, or how her lips would part on a gasp or a sigh as he touched her or she surrendered to the throes of an orgasm.

Now she was standing in front of him, setting him free when he didn't want to be freed. Not knowing that even when she did, he would still be tied to her.

For the rest of his days.

'You were there at the right time to help me take some of those first steps towards finding myself. I'd have got there eventually on my own, but I'm glad you were there anyway.' She glanced at him from the corner of her eye and smiled. 'Even if you were such a pain in the neck at the beginning.'

He dug deep and managed a smile in return. 'That goes both ways.'

Musical laughter spilled out and filled the room for a brief moment. 'Yes, I guess it does.'

Seeming to understand that a truce had been made, she stepped closer to him, her head tilted to one side as she continued to look at him from the corner of her eye and below lowered lashes. 'Sometimes there's just a right place and a right time for something to happen, don't you think?'

'Yes, I think that.'

'We might never have met.'

'That's true. You've lived three streets away from a gym I've part-owned for five years and we never met before.'

'And yet, when I was ready to go out into the world, there you were.'

Rory's heart thundered in his chest as she stepped even closer, her steps measured, controlled, while her mouth stayed curved up at the edges and she eyed him from beneath her lashes. Her head tilted back a little when she was right in front of him.

'I know what doing what you do means to you, even if it doesn't seem real to me in the here and now. I see it in your eyes when you talk about the people you work with and I know how natural a thing it is for you to take control, and assume responsibility for others. I wouldn't change a single thing, because it's all part of who you are.' She shook her head. 'But I won't let you take responsibility for the decisions I make. *They're mine.* Right or wrong, they're my choices to make; they help make me who *I* am, and who I'm going to be after this. I'm ready to go explore the world. It's just something I have to do.'

She paused, took a breath, smiled a melancholy smile. 'There's no sad ending here. We just go in different directions; that's all. Sort of like we did before, only better, because we had this and we get to keep it.'

He swallowed hard and her eyes dropped to his throat.

Every cell in his body was calling out for him to tell her how he felt. How walking away from her would be the toughest thing he'd ever had to do. Even tougher than watching a car bounce into the air in front of him had been. Maybe even tougher than dragging a friend from that car, seeing with his own eyes the damage that had been done, knowing there wasn't a single thing he wouldn't have risked to stop it from happening.

They were facts that he had no control over, even though he had felt he should have had. It had been a risk they had all known they were taking, so they had prepared for it. As best they could.

But there had been no way Rory could ever have prepared

for Cara Sheehan. How did anyone prepare for how they would feel, how all consuming it was when they finally found the love of a lifetime?

But even though, in that instant, he would have tried his damnedest to adjust his lifestyle for her, he knew it would make him exactly what Connor had called him a few hours ago.

A selfish bastard.

Cara needed to make this trip of hers, to go out and do all the things she wanted to do and leave behind all the things that had hidden her away. And Rory knew he had to let her do that. Because he wouldn't hold her back when she'd already come so far.

Any more than he could have lived with himself if something happened to any of the men he had left behind in his absence if he was selfish enough to quit on them for his own chance at happiness. He would always carry the guilt. There would always be a doubt in his mind.

When someone loved someone as much as he loved Cara, they wanted them to have what was best for them. And sometimes that meant accepting there was no choice but to let them go.

She was right. They had different lives. And there was no win-win solution that he could see in the here and now.

So he looked at the ceiling and swore viciously.

When he looked back down she was staring at him with a million questions in her eyes.

So he lifted his hands, his fingers sliding around her neck and into her hair, thumbs on the fine line of her jaw, and he took a deep breath. 'Do you have any idea how amazing a woman you are?'

Her smile was tremulous. 'I had some help with that.'

'No.' He shook his head. 'It was always there.'

Her eyes shimmered again when he couldn't manage to hold the tremor from his husky tone. She blinked hard, and a lone tear shone on her lower lashes before it streaked along her cheek.

Rory brushed it away with the tip of his thumb and leaned his forehead against hers. 'Don't you dare cry.'

She sniffed. 'I'm not.'

'You're such a bad liar.'

'And you're still a pain in the butt.'

He chuckled. 'So.'

'So?' She sniffed again and her long lashes rose as she looked up into the eyes so close to hers.

'So I guess maybe I should see about some more of these terrific memories…'

'That sounds like a plan to me.'

'Can't have you forgetting how amazing *I* am while you're off trotting the globe.'

'Yeah, because once you're gone it'll take me about five minutes to forget you otherwise.'

'Nah.' He dipped his mouth to hers and gently brushed over her lips. 'Once you've had the best there's no going back.'

Her arms snaked around his waist and she pulled her body tight in against his, her heart beating against his, in synch beat for beat.

And Rory untangled his fingers from her hair, circled his arms around her upper body, holding her even tighter, even closer. As if by doing so he could somehow absorb a part of her into himself. And keep it.

A swap for the part he had just given away of himself by letting her go. Even for a while.

If she was his, then she'd come back to him. And he'd find a way of meeting her in the middle. He'd *find* a way. He had to.

Even if, while he held her against him, he had no idea how to find a solution that would satisfy all the people he was responsible for. And for the first time ever, *including himself.*

CHAPTER SIXTEEN

RORY SAVED THE best memory for last. Even though, for Cara, nothing would ever be able to erase the agony of letting him go.

It just went to prove that the old saying of being forewarned meant you were forearmed wasn't true at all. Being forewarned wasn't a way of escaping the pain to come. It was more like premeditated grief. And there was just no way to avoid the agony of grief. It was something that had to be experienced, worked through, accepted as being beyond a person's control, then carried while moving on.

It started with an envelope through her door.

'Meet me in the pool. Keys are for front doors.' Brief and to the point. And yet the simple scrawled words sent an expectant tremor through her entire body. They had history with that pool, after all. And she knew that he was flying out soon. Not that she knew an exact day or time. But it was soon.

Inside the darkened gym she found a light on in the changing rooms. A bikini. Another note.

'Thought I'd take a peek at what the rest of the world will get to see.'

Even though she'd actually been kidding about the bikini part, she put it on. Because she was dressing up for Rory, the man who had seen her naked more times in the last couple of weeks than she had probably seen herself, ever. There was no self-consciousness left in her where he was concerned. And she smiled when she looked at herself in a mirror before she went to the pool.

Yep, six weeks of varying physical activities had certainly done a lot to tone her up.

When she opened the door to the pool her breath caught. It was dark inside; no overhead lights on. So that the only light in the large, steam-filled room was the underwater lighting, and the flickering light from what looked like hundreds of candles.

The surface of the water rippled as Rory slid through it in a long-armed crawl. He did his trademark perfect underwater turn at the other end, looked up about halfway back towards her. Then, when he reached the end where she stood, he folded his arms on the tiles and looked up at her; smiling *that* smile.

He was the sexiest man on the planet.

'You took your time. I'm thirty laps ahead of you.'

Cara stared at him for a long time. His hair was plastered to his head, dark curls of it all across his forehead and curling over his ears; water dripping off the ends and running down his face. And his fathomless eyes sparkled at her in the flickering light.

Definitely the sexiest man on the planet.

'Did you rob a candle shop today?' She quirked an eyebrow at him, a half smile playing on her lips.

Still smiling, he looked around, nodding slowly so that more droplets of water fell from his hair. 'It felt like it. Do you have any idea how long it takes to light this many of the damn things? I burnt my fingers about twenty times.'

'It's as well you had some water around then.'

'I plan ahead.' His gaze returned to her, caressing every feature on her face before, ever so slowly, making an open study of her body.

And Cara felt every single place he looked tingle and come to life, as if he were physically touching her. Her breasts grew swollen and heavy, her nipples strained against the triangles of material. The muscles of her stomach tightened, signalling the beginning of a familiar chain reaction that began with a knot of anticipation forming low in her abdomen. And heat moved in waves over her, building sensual flames that licked up inside her.

It had taken a while for her to figure it out. But somewhere along the way she had recognized that it all came down to anticipation of Rory. Not the act itself. Not the wondrous magical release that inevitably came at the end.

No, it wasn't just what he could do to her with fingers, hands, tongue or whispered words, or how he could have her completely abandon herself in his arms.

It was so many other things that made up the whole heavenly result. Like the anticipation of him smiling at her, or consuming her with his eyes. The sound of his deep voice as he talked to her, challenged her or shared thoughts with her; the low rumble of his laughter.

She looked forward to all of those things when she wasn't with him and wanted him all the more when they were right in front of her.

It was all the little things that added up to his being, for her, the sexiest man on the planet.

She lifted her chin with the confidence of a woman who knew she was equally sexually attractive to the man she desired, holding her arms out to the sides, making a slow turn for his delectation.

And his eyes were a shade darker when she looked at him again. 'You're beautiful, Cara Sheehan.'

Cara rolled her eyes and grinned. 'Shucks.'

Rory held an arm out to her, his palm upwards, empty, waiting for her hand to fill it. So she walked over and sat down on the tiles, slipping her hand into his and allowing him to pull her forwards, warm water sliding up her body, and washing over her sensitive breasts.

He pressed his body in against hers so that she was trapped against the tiles. Kissing her slowly, as if she might break in his hold; starting at her forehead and then working his way over the arch of each eyebrow, closing each eye, then the tip of her nose, each corner of her mouth. Then, finally, deeper, full-mouthed, hot, wet kisses that drew low moans from her throat as she let her legs rise in the water and wrap around his waist.

With a little upward push he had her half out of the water, her back arching over the edge so that her breasts were offered up to his mouth. And he stayed there for a long time, taking for ever to untie the minute strings behind her back and under her hair, his mouth and teeth moving from breast to breast.

They moved out from the edge of the pool, legs tangling in the water while they finished removing scraps of clothing, laughing along the way. Then they spun round in slow, never-ending circles, dancing around each other's bodies and kissing and kissing. *Just kissing;* bodies floating together, apart, then together again.

It was the most beautiful thing Cara had ever known or thought she ever would.

But kissing wasn't enough.

They floated to the shallow end, feet hitting bottom, until her back was once more against the tiles. Then Rory kissed down her neck, spent more time on each breast, drew each nipple into his mouth in turn and suckled until she was tangling her fingers in his hair and arching closer to encourage him.

He raised his head, waited until her chin tilted forwards and her eyes met his. Then held the eye contact while he smoothed her wet hair back off her shoulders, his fingers tracing her collar-bone, the rounded curves of her shoulders, down over each breast, where he cupped and gently kneaded, his thumbs brushing back and forth over her now aching, distended nipples.

So Cara echoed the touch, her fingertips starting higher, on the curve of his mouth, then over the line of his jaw, down the strong column of his neck. She traced his collar-bone, smoothed her palms over the tight wall of his chest, circled her fingernails in his chest hair.

And all the while she stared into his midnight eyes with slow blinking of her long lashes.

'You really are beautiful, you know.'

Her mouth curled into a smile at his hoarsely whispered

words. She felt beautiful. When he looked at her that way, touched her that way, she felt like the most beautiful, worshipped woman on the planet.

I love you.

It was on the tip of her tongue, as if her heart had willed the words there without her having to think it.

She swallowed, forced the confession away. And moved her hands around his hard torso to press herself closer to him, her lips touching the skin below his ear where she whispered, 'You make me feel beautiful.'

She could still feel his hands on her, could still remember how they spent what felt like hours both in and eventually out of the water, until she was beneath him on the long cushions he threw off the pool loungers.

She could still feel her back arching upwards as his mouth worked its way in a torturous trail from her breasts to her stomach, and lower. Could remember the cries she made when he parted her thighs and sought her core with his tongue. How his hands on her hips had held her in place while he brought her to the edge, and stopped, then closer, and stopped.

Until she was almost sobbing from the agony.

Then the muscles on his back strained beneath her hands as he slid slowly into her body, sheathing himself in her, filling her with his hard length.

Cara could remember looking up at his face as she lifted her legs and wrapped them around his, her hands on the small of his back, urging him on. He had looked tortured, as if he was fighting a battle for self-control. His breathing laboured, his dark brows creased down over heavy eyelids.

And she was so close. It would take so little for him to send her over the edge, spiralling into temporary bliss.

She tilted her hips up and down, forcing him deeper and smiling in satisfaction as he surged down with her, deeper again.

'I could spend for ever inside you. But I don't think I can hold out much longer.'

Cara smiled up at him. 'Fast and hard would definitely work for me at this stage.'

And with a deep groan he accepted the invitation, thrusting into her over and over and over; so deep inside that Cara didn't know where she ended and he began.

She dug her fingernails into his skin, arched upwards to meet each thrust so that his pelvic bone rubbed against her clitoris. And even before she saw him arch back his head, a long, low moan signalling his climax, she was already clamping around him as her body fell apart.

And then silence. And kissing. Slow, soft kisses and husky murmurs. While Cara tried to tell him she loved him without saying it aloud.

But it wasn't that the lovemaking and the closeness had been the only best part of the final memory. Because they then shared a picnic on the gym floor: bottles of water and energy bars Rory raided from the machines down the hall. They lazed about, hair still wet, while they joked and teased and told stories from their childhood.

Cara learnt more about his family; about the father who had tried to support his huge family on the salary of a night-time security guard on the docks. How Rory had had all the best clothes as the eldest and tallest, while the rest of them had had 'hand-me-downs'. About the *Fighting Flanaghans:* four brothers scrapping with each other every five minutes, then scrapping with anyone outside of the family who would dare say anything against any one of them.

She listened with better understanding as he told her about going into the army; taking those first steps into a well-paid job so he could bring security to the kids who were younger than him. Eyes shining with pride as he talked about the ones who had done well, who didn't need his helping hand any more.

They had all done their part to hold their family together, especially after their dad had died. And Cara could see even more of the wealth of caring he had for other people. With his workmates, he was just doing what he had always done. He was looking out for them.

He wouldn't abandon them any quicker than he had the family he loved so much. To him, the risks he took were worth the gains.

But she couldn't help aching for that kind of love from him. What would it take to bring a man like him home, to convince him that, if he asked her to, she would wait however long it took for him to decide to leave danger behind? To build the kind of family for himself that he'd had growing up, that he had gone out alone to help support? With midnight-eyed, tousle-haired boys who would scrap with each other and anyone who dared say anything bad about any one of them.

It was so vivid an image it felt as if it pulled her bones from her body, leaving her a big pile of mush.

How she *loved* him!

'Miss? Can I help you?'

If she had known when he walked her through the streets as the sun came up that it would be the last time she saw him before he left, then she would more than likely have told him then how much she loved him.

She should have *known* it was the last time.

Because he held her so tight for so long at her front door, whispering about the memories they'd made and how he hoped she would never forget them, because he knew he wouldn't.

She was so torn when he walked away. So keen to sleep for a few hours so she could block out the building agony and dream about the magic. To waste away a few hours so she could see him again. When she eventually drifted off, she slept late, woke invigorated and excited, ate a hearty, healthy breakfast to keep her strength up for their next encounter.

And she still didn't feel anything was wrong.

It took her to walk to the gym, her steps light and fast, before she found her way to the grief she'd been waiting for.

'Miss Sheehan? Erm, Cara?'

She turned at the sound of her name, a bright smile in place. Looked up into a face so like Rory's, but different, 'Hi. You must be Connor.'

Connor nodded, shook her hand when she offered it. While Cara was struck by how much he was like his elder brother: same coloured eyes, same dark hair, same height. Same way of avoiding looking into her eyes when something was difficult to say…

'Rory asked me to give you this. We had a bit of an argument about it, actually.' He took a deep breath. 'It cost him, Cara. I just thought you should know that. If anything could have brought him home for good, it would have been you.'

And there it was: another envelope. Her heart automatically hoping it was another memory in the making when she already knew it wasn't.

'My flight is today.'

'Miss? Do you need me to have someone paged for you?'

She ran all the way to the nearest taxi rank, reading the rest in the moving car, while she tried to catch her breath and calm the agonizing beating of her heart.

'There's no way to say goodbye to you. I've tried and I just can't do it. So I said goodbye last night. I have to do the right thing, honey; it's what I do. So that means I have to think about what's best for both of us right now, and for the men who rely on me. If they weren't there I wouldn't even be leaving. I hope you know that.

Live life large on that trip, Cara, do you hear me? Well, within reason. Because I don't want you to forget me.

I won't forget a single thing about you. I promise.'

'Miss?'

It took the hand on her arm for her to focus. She looked down at it blindly, through a haze. Then she looked up at the concerned face of the security guard.

He smiled encouragingly at her. 'Can I help you?'

She looked around at the crowds of people, a sea of strangers all making their way to and from their destinations; caught sight of a woman running into the arms of a man. And her heart shattered into billions of tiny, irreparable pieces.

He was gone.

'Are you meeting someone, or are you lost maybe?'

Her eyes went back up to the banks of screens above her and she shook her head as the tears came again, streaming down her already soaked face. This was so stupid. She didn't even know a flight number or where he was flying to. And if he'd wanted her there he'd have told her he did.

She shook her head again. 'No.'

But she *felt* lost. *Utterly.* She should have told him, just the one time. Even if he hadn't felt the same way, he'd have known. She'd have known he knew.

The lump in her throat hurt when she swallowed. Maybe it *was* better his way, maybe he had been right. Because she couldn't have said goodbye, either. And if he had felt even the smallest iota of the all-consuming love she felt for him, he would have told her, wouldn't he?

This way she didn't have to put herself through that awful moment of seeing in his eyes that he didn't feel what she felt. It would have been a memory that would have tainted all the others. And she just couldn't lose them.

They were all she had left.

'Here.'

She looked down at the proffered handkerchief and managed a watery smile. 'Thank you. That's very kind.'

'Airports are awful places. There's always someone saying goodbye to a loved one—' he pushed the peaked cap back on his head, revealing flattened grey hair '—but you stand here long enough and eventually they all come back.'

'You must see a lot of broken hearts.'

He smiled. 'My auld ma always said if you love someone,

you'll let them go and if they're meant for you, they'll come back again. Remember that, and it'll get you by; that's what she said.'

More tears welled in her eyes. 'Did she mention how much the letting-go sucks?'

Because it did. It *really* did.

CHAPTER SEVENTEEN

'THERE YOU ARE! Goodness don't you look fabulous?' Joyce leaned in and gave her a kiss on the cheek. 'It's an absolute madhouse. Could you get parked anywhere close?'

Cara smiled broadly. 'Yes, and less than half a mile away, which I thought was pretty good myself.'

And she had thanked the stars above for it, truth be told. She hadn't wanted to look across the street and see the house that Rory owned. Coming home to her house, and all its associated memories, had been agony enough, thanks all the same.

Whoever had said 'time heals all wounds' needed to be tied to a pole and beaten to death with a million broken hearts. *Big fat liar!* They'd probably been a hundred years old and had married the first guy they met in preschool.

'Where's—?'

But Joyce was already down the hall, welcoming another set of late arrivals. How her parents could have this many friends stunned her. Mind you, Joyce would always be ready and willing to chat to each and every one of them.

The thought made her smile affectionately at her stepmother. It was funny how sometimes, in order to truly appreciate your family, you had to go to another country for a while.

Cara had missed them. She really had. And much as she had loved seeing all the places she had only dreamt of as a child, she had known it was time to come home.

She knew what she needed to know. There was no point in trying to make changes she couldn't make. She loved Rory; would do for the rest of her life. And despite the pain that accompanied that, the gaping hole in her soul, she wouldn't change it, even if she could. She never wanted to forget how it felt to have had that, even just for a short while. Many people went through life with less.

Suddenly she was surrounded, a flurry of squealing women kissing her cheeks and hugging her in turn.

'Oh my God—look at you! Have you seen her, Laura? She looks gorgeous! So tanned and relaxed.'

Cara blinked madly as she tried to put all of them in focus, her eyes drawn to one of her stepsisters as she turned her around by the shoulders.

'I'm so jealous of that tan! Is it an all-over?'

Cara laughed. 'I'm not answering that.'

'*It is!* You gorgeous, wicked thing!' She giggled infectiously as Cara found herself joining in. 'And I'm so borrowing that dress. It's sexy as hell!'

Laura took her turn in the queue to kiss and hug. 'It's about bloody time you got back. We've all missed you like mad! I sincerely hope that you're done with the travelling.'

'Yes, I'm home now.' Where all the best memories were.

The other half of the dynamic steptwins appeared at her side and winked. 'And I would be, too, if I was in your shoes.' She added a kiss to Cara's already numb cheek. 'Aren't you the secretive one?'

Huh? All right, twelve hours sleep obviously hadn't cured her jet lag, then.

'I'm sure she would have told us all if it wasn't meant as a surprise.'

Her eyes went to Laura's beaming face again and she opened her mouth in a perfect circle. 'Oh. You mean the new book. Yeah, they're very excited about it.'

'You have a new book? Another *The Right To…*? What's this one called?'

Cara frowned in confusion. She had gone away and everyone

had obviously taken up drugs in her absence. 'It doesn't have a title confirmed yet.'

'Another diet one? I liked them the best, though the one about bottled-up anger was hilarious. *The Right To Scream Out Loud.* I gave it to Ryan when we came back off honeymoon so he could understand why once a month I lock myself in the bathroom and scream for five minutes. Didn't want to scare him off once I'd finally got hold of him.'

'No-o.' Cara was still a mite bemused. 'Not a diet book. This one is about allowing yourself to be happy.'

'Any wonder you wrote that now!' The second twin pushed back to the front. 'I'd be writing about the right to stay indoors indefinitely if I were you…'

Everyone laughed. Except Cara.

'Am I missing something?'

Joyce was back. Her voice sing-songing as she pushed into the fray. 'Isn't this lovely? Cara's finally home! We've all missed her terribly, haven't we, girls?'

There was a chorus of varying agreements. Then Joyce reached a hand out and squeezed Cara's arm. 'I meant to tell you, your dad is out in the conservatory with that young man of yours. Well, they were five minutes ago.' Lifting the hand, she waved it back and forth. 'Deep in discussion about the merits of central heating last I checked. All terribly technical for me, I'm afraid. Now, does everyone have a drink? Refill, Laura?'

'Hang on—'

'Oh, you don't have a glass, darling! Your usual red or have you gone all cocktails since you left? I do love all those bendy straws and bright colours, don't you?'

'What young man of mine?'

It was like watching a sitcom from halfway through. And Cara felt distinctly as if everyone else had been watching when she hadn't. She didn't have a young man! Not any more anyway. And the only one her family had met in the last while was halfway across the world now.

There was another chorus of laughter.

But Cara still wasn't laughing. 'No, seriously, what young man?'

'Why, that lovely neighbour of ours, of course! Silly girl. We all know now. He's been jumpy all night waiting for you to get here!'

She froze. Her heart stopped beating. And she suddenly couldn't speak.

'Cara?' Laura bent her face closer, her voice concerned. 'Are you all right?'

She found her voice, croaked and low as it was. 'Excuse me.'

It took for ever for her to push her way through the crowd. Dozens of relatives she hadn't seen in years clamouring to tell her how gorgeous she looked and to mention how lovely her young man was. So that by the time the glass of the conservatory came into view she felt dizzy, a little bit nauseous, and the room was so hot she thought she might pass out.

Her feet grew heavy as she got closer; she heard her father's deep rumble of laughter and beyond that all she could hear was the thunder of her heartbeat in her ears.

She tilted her head forwards, and peered tentatively round the edge.

Eyes as dark as a midnight sky speckled with bright stars rose and locked with hers. And she gasped as he smiled *that* smile.

Rory was *here?*

This couldn't be happening. She was still sleeping off her jet lag; that *had* to be it. Yes. She was still at home asleep, surrounded by memories of him there, and her mind was putting together a happy ending while she slept.

'There she is!' Her father stepped forward and reached for her hand, drawing her into the room. 'Let's get a better look at you, sweetheart. My, aren't you looking well?'

He ushered her to do a twirl, as he used to do when she was a kid and was wearing her new school uniform on the first day of term. And Cara, in her hypnotic state, slowly twirled on automatic pilot, her eyes fixed on Rory's as she moved. He couldn't be here!

'Well, she was worth the wait, wasn't she, Rory, my boy? I

can't remember when she looked so beautiful. She's just like her mother, you know.' He smiled down at her with glittering eyes and kissed her on the cheek before adding in a husky voice, 'You'll make a very lovely bride, just like she did.'

'*What?*'

The words had been the first thing to drag her eyes from Rory's hypnotic gaze—*at speed.* But as the meaning sank in she looked away from the glow of pride on her father's face and back to the wide grin on Rory's face.

'You.' She pointed a finger at him, her words slow and deliberately calm. 'Kitchen. *Right now!*'

He didn't look the least bit fazed, damn him.

'Okay.' He even patted her Dad on the back before he left. 'I'll see you in a minute, James.'

James beamed in response. 'Look forward to it, son.'

Son?

One step and his large frame was in front of her; a smile still on his face as he held an arm out in invitation. 'After you, honey.'

Cara seriously contemplated murder; even while the blood rushed faster through her veins and every fibre of her being shouted with joy at his being there.

But before she gave a hint of how happy she was to see him she really needed to know what the *hell* was going on!

It took nearly as long to get back through the living room as it had the first time. And it was tougher with Rory's hand planted possessively in the small of her back; and what felt like dozens of people beaming at the 'happy couple'.

Every damn one of them relatives that Rory knew on a first name basis!

The kitchen wasn't empty, either. And Cara almost screamed with frustration. 'Hello, Auntie Doris.'

'Cara! There you are at last. My goodness, don't you look well?' Another kiss, another cheek later. 'You're so slim, though—haven't you been eating? Here, have some of my chicken.'

A paper plate was thrust in her hand.

Then her aunt beamed upwards. 'Rory. You'll take more. I know how much you love my chicken.'

'I'd love to, Auntie Doris—' he rubbed his stomach while Cara glared at him '—but I've already had two plates. You feed me too well.'

'Nonsense.' She batted his arm and her eyelashes at the same time. 'A strapping boy like you needs his food.'

'Auntie Doris, could we have a minute?'

'Oh, of course, darling! You two love-birds won't have had your reunion yet. I'll guard the door for you.'

She winked at Rory on the way past and he was still laughing as Cara threw her plate of chicken in the sink and rounded on him.

'What the hell is going on? What are you doing at my parents' anniversary party? How come every single member of my family knows you? And why are you even here? You're supposed to be off dodging bullets in some desert somew—'

His mouth stole the last words from her, his body pressing in against hers and trapping her against the counter. And for the life of her, Cara could think of nothing better to do but kiss him back.

Oh, Lord, how she'd missed him! It was like having a part of her soul that had been missing returned to her, so that she felt whole again for the first time in over three months. *This* was what she remembered most.

His warm mouth on hers, stealing the air from her lungs as her blood boiled.

She moaned, wrapped her arms around his neck and drew him as close as she could get him through their layers of clothing. Her lips parted, his tongue driving in and dancing with hers.

And the deep knot of need in her abdomen almost doubled her over.

No, no, hang on! He hadn't answered any of her questions. He couldn't just be there after three months and kiss her sense-less and not give her an explanation. She was a confident, capable, worldly woman, for crying out loud!

She needed more than mind-blowingly great sex this time!

After all, she'd just spent over three long, lonely months grieving for the loss of him…

'Mmmff—' She struggled against him, moving her arms from round his neck so she could push against his chest. 'No, Rory, wait!'

'God, how I've missed you.' It was practically a groan against her lips. And when she opened her eyes he was looking down at her with such an expression of agony that she almost gave in. *Almost*.

She pushed again, hard. Fully prepared to stomp on his toes if she had to. 'Wait. Rory! Damn it. Would you *stop?*'

The shaking of her head from side to side eventually forced him to lift his mouth from hers. But he didn't move away. His hard body remained pressed all along the length of hers, his rapidly growing erection tight against her stomach, her breasts crushed against his chest.

And Cara moaned again from the sheer temptation of him. 'I really need you to give me some space for a minute here. *Seriously.*'

His deep voice rumbled out on a note of complaint. 'I've given you plenty of space for three bloody months. I'm not giving you any more. It's been hell waiting for you to come home.'

'*What?*' She stared at him in blank astonishment. 'What do you mean, you've been giving me space for three months? *You left!*'

'Only because I had to.' He blinked thick lashes at her as he leaned forward again, errant strands of dark hair dropping across his forehead. 'You knew that. But I had to let you do what you needed to do. I couldn't hold you back from finding out what you really needed.'

Cara's fingers itched to brush his hair back, so she balled them into fists against his chest. 'And what exactly was it you thought I needed?'

'Me. You just needed a little time to figure it out.'

'*You moron!* I knew that before you left! I didn't need to take a damn trip all over the place to know that!'

'You were determined to take it, though.'

Oh, this was what she got for not telling him the whole truth, was it? More than three months of agony for trying to save him from knowing how much his leaving would hurt her.

'I took it so I wouldn't be here when you were gone! I knew how much it would kill me being in the same places we'd been when you weren't there. And that damn well included my own house!'

The sparks in Rory's eyes flared. 'Cara Sheehan!' There was a note of shocked outrage in his voice. 'You *lied* to me?'

She felt an unwanted warmth crawl over her cheeks. 'I wasn't going to give you a guilt complex about leaving when you'd made it very clear from the start that you weren't the stay-at-home type!'

'And still, you didn't think to take the chance and just be honest with me.'

'Oh, I thought about it.' She laughed a little frantically. 'I thought about it so much that I even chased after you to the airport to tell you how I felt! *That's* how much I thought about it. But you were so busy running off into the sunset that you didn't bother telling me what flight you were on and I ended up crying like a lunatic in the middle of Dublin Airport!'

Rory's mouth curled into an affectionate smile, a look of wonder in his eyes. 'You did?'

'Yes, I *did.* I still have a security guard's hanky.'

'I didn't know.' The words came out on a hoarse whisper as his head lowered again. '*Sweetheart—*'

This time her laughter held a more sarcastic edge.

'O-h-h, no, you don't. Get off me this minute. We're not done!' She pushed hard.

But he simply raised his head and stood his ground.

Cara muffled a scream. 'If you don't move back I swear I'm going right out there and telling my entire family that you are some kind of maniac who's been trailing me for months. I'll tell them you escaped from an asylum.'

'Your entire family loves me already. They won't believe you. Since you weren't here it made sense to be around people who reminded me of you. So they're on *my* side.'

She lifted a hand from his chest and pointed a finger past him. 'Back. *Right now.*'

'I love it when you go all bossy on me. Have I ever mentioned how sexy it is?'

When she growled he laughed, held a palm up and moved back. 'Okay. Fine. But I'm not staying over here for long.'

A little distance helped. A very, very small amount. It gave her a moment to straighten her clothes, to smooth her hair into place, and to take a deep breath before she looked at him again.

He was smiling *that* smile.

'Stop that and tell me what you're doing here.'

'Waiting for you.'

She scowled. 'For how long?'

'Three weeks.'

'What happened to your work?'

'Ah.' He glanced away for a moment, then back, catching Cara's widening gaze just in time to stop her imagination from kicking into overdrive. 'I didn't get hurt. Not this time.'

'But something happened, didn't it?'

'Yes. We got hit again.' He clamped down the deep-seated need to hold her in his arms as he told her. Because she wasn't hiding her anguish so well this time round. And his heart swelled that she cared so deeply. *Thank God.*

There had been a time or two the last few weeks when he had felt self-doubt wash over him, and worse than that, *fear.* What if, by giving her the space to do what she'd had to do, he had unwittingly allowed someone else to work their way into her heart?

He'd never have recovered if that had happened. Because she was his, just as he was hers; no question about it in his mind.

'No one got hurt. Unless you count the ringing in my ears for four days afterwards.'

'And ringing ears suddenly had you racing home to wait for me in the bosom of my family, did they?'

'No.' He could deal with her sarcasm. He'd done it plenty of times before. And he knew she only did it when she was scared, or hiding. It was her defence shield.

'What brought me racing home was that the only thing I could think of when it happened was you. You were right at the front of my mind. Not whether or not I was hurt, or one of my team was hurt. Just you. And coming back to you. You ruined me for my job, Cara; I couldn't do it any more. I got too cautious, you see; my sense of self-preservation kicked in. And too cautious is almost as bad as reckless in my job. I couldn't put those guys in danger just because I wanted to stay safe for you.'

Her breathing hitched, her eyes shimmering. 'But your job is such a big part of who you are. I can't let you give that up for me. You'd never forgive yourself if you weren't there to help them.'

'And I am helping them. I'm just doing it a different way. A way that lets me stay home more, keeps me out of the danger zone—' he stuck out his bottom lip and shrugged his shoulders before adding '—and stops me constantly reflex ducking so that my adorable big self can get back to you in one piece.'

For the first time he could remember, she let his arrogance slide unchecked. 'What kind of a job lets you do all that?'

'You see, that's the best part.' He grinned. 'I get to help find new wet-behind-the-ears to train up and then I get to pass on all my expertise at training camps in Turkey a few times a year. That way the lads get fully-trained mini-me's to keep them out of trouble.'

There was a distinct silence as Cara stared up at him. It took a moment. Then she smiled, her heart shimmering in her eyes. 'And you get to stay home the rest of the time?'

Rory nodded firmly. 'And bug the hell out of my brothers while we expand the gym business.'

It was too good to be true.

But one look into his gleaming eyes was enough to confirm he was more than happy with the solution he'd found. Which left just one more question before she could surrender herself to the sheer joy of it all.

'And why exactly does my entire family think we're getting married?'

'Because we are. Aren't we?'

It was the brief look of insecurity in his eyes that did her in. How could she not want to spend for ever with him?

Cara's mouth curled into a smile. 'It's nice to be asked, you know.'

'Ah, but I know how stubborn you can be sometimes. So I figured if it was a done deal you'd have more of a problem turning me down.'

She tilted her head to one side. 'And what if I still say no, since *you're* being so bossy?'

'Then I'm going to have to spend a few weeks persuading you to say yes. I'm fully prepared for twenty-four-hour shifts, seven days a week, if that's what it takes. You're stuck with me now.'

And that was probably the most romantic thing he'd ever said to her. 'I suppose you have the church booked, my dress picked out and all my bridesmaids on stand-by?'

'That bit you can do on your own.'

'Like hell I will. It takes two to make a marriage Rory Flanaghan.'

'Yes.' His eyes darkened to the fathomless black that warmed her soul and turned her mind to making love with him as soon as humanly possible. 'I'd heard that. Two equals. Two people who don't want to be without each other ever again. So, will you marry me?'

Cara could feel the tears building in the backs of her eyes again as he single-handedly erased the past few months of agony from her memory. This was what she would remember the rest of her life. The day her husband had proposed to her. And she had said yes.

'Yes I'll marry you. You know I will. You could have asked me three months ago and I'd have said yes. And I'd have waited for as long as it took for you to come home.'

Yep. A girl just didn't forget something like this. The way that his eyes glowed across at her as the flicker of a doubt was finally removed. It was always the happiest moments that overshadowed the bad in the end, wasn't it?

Rory pushed off the counter facing her and smiled a smile that even outshone *that* smile, because this time there was nothing to hide. 'So are you going to say it first or am I?'

She laughed joyously. 'I love you. I loved you before you left and I will love you 'til the day I die. Was that what you meant?'

He nodded, his eyes shining. 'That's what I meant.'

'Then what are you doing all the way over there?'

He closed the gap between them in one swift move, his hands framing her face, thumbs touching the corners of her mouth as he leaned in closer, his voice husky. 'I'm not going to say I love you. Because those words aren't big enough for how I feel about you. You're the first thing I've ever needed for myself, Cara. Not for my family or for the people I worked with. Just for me. I *need* you. I don't want to be without you. That's why I let you go back then, even though it killed me. I had to be sure you felt the same way.'

He took a ragged breath. 'You see, if you love someone you have to let them go, so they can come back to you. That way you know they're yours. *For ever.*'

Cara smiled up at him, her heart bursting out of her chest as she stood up on her tiptoes to bring her mouth to his. 'I heard something like that somewhere. And I am yours. *For ever.* I already wasted half my life waiting for you to find me in the first place.'

Their mouths tangled again, touched and parted, the kiss a gentler one compared to the initial frantic greeting they'd made only minutes before. But within seconds of him moving his hands from her face to draw her into the length of his body, where she curved in and fitted into every place designed solely for her, Rory found her dragging her mouth free. He opened his heavy eyelids and gazed down at her; his Cara, his friend, his lover, *his;* for ever.

He was home at last.

And she smiled a smile that told him that went both ways, before a thought crossed her expressive eyes and she frowned while informing him, 'I'm not living across the street from my parents.'

Rory laughed out loud. 'How about we talk about it later? *Much later.* We have a party to escape and three months of catching up to do.'

'Oh, I'm with you on the catching up. But they'll hear me from over there, so we're moving. I want to make all the noise in the world with you, and we wouldn't want to ruin their great opinion of you as the perfect son-in-law, now would we?'

He groaned loudly. 'All right, you win. It's only a house. And I don't give a damn where we live. I've already got everything I need right here in my arms.'

Lord, how she loved him!

'You really are the best.'

'Yeah, I know. I just won you, didn't I?'

There was no arguing that really. 'Mmm. You're still a pain in the neck, though.'

'Yep.' With another loud, smacking kiss, he stepped away, yanked open the door, looked round the edge and held out his hand for her. 'No Auntie Doris. Get ready to run.'

Cara glanced down at his large hand, then up into his dark eyes. That great plan for a new life had gone pretty damn well, hadn't it?

So she smiled and placed her hand in his.

'I'm *more* than ready. And now that we've got everything sorted out, I don't need to hold back *anything* any more, do I?'

She stepped closer and looked up at him. 'I'm a very highly sexually charged woman, you know.'

Rory groaned and tugged hard on her hand. 'How fast can you run?'

HARLEQUIN Presents

Don't miss the brilliant
new novel from

Natalie Rivers

**featuring a dark, dangerous
and decadent Italian!**

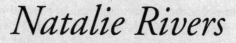

THE SALVATORE
MARRIAGE DEAL

Available June 2008
Book #2735

*Look out for more books
from Natalie Rivers coming soon,
only in Harlequin Presents!*

www.eHarlequin.com   HP12735

HARLEQUIN® *Presents*

What do you look for in a guy?
Charisma. Sex appeal. Confidence.
A body to die for. Well, look no further
this series has men with all this and more!
And now that they've met the women in these novels,
there is one thing on everyone's mind….

NIGHTS *of* PASSION

One night is never enough!

**The guys know what they want
and how they're going to get it!**

Don't miss:

HIS MISTRESS
BY ARRANGEMENT
by

Natalie Anderson

Available June 2008.

*Look out for more Nights of Passion,
coming soon in Harlequin Presents!*

www.eHarlequin.com   HPI2737

REQUEST YOUR FREE BOOKS!

HARLEQUIN® *Presents*®

2 FREE NOVELS PLUS 2 FREE GIFTS!

PASSION GUARANTEED SEDUCTION

YES! Please send me 2 FREE Harlequin Presents® novels and my 2 FREE gifts (gifts are worth about $10). After receiving them, if I don't wish to receive any more books, I can return the shipping statement marked "cancel". If I don't cancel, I will receive 6 brand-new novels every month and be billed just $4.05 per book in the U.S. or $4.74 per book in Canada, plus 25¢ shipping and handling per book and applicable taxes, if any*. That's a savings of close to 15% off the cover price! I understand that accepting the 2 free books and gifts places me under no obligation to buy anything. I can always return a shipment and cancel at any time. Even if I never buy another book, the two free books and gifts are mine to keep forever.

106 HDN ERRW 306 HDN ERRL

Name	(PLEASE PRINT)	
Address		Apt. #
City	State/Prov.	Zip/Postal Code

Signature (if under 18, a parent or guardian must sign)

Mail to the **Harlequin Reader Service:**
IN U.S.A.: P.O. Box 1867, Buffalo, NY 14240-1867
IN CANADA: P.O. Box 609, Fort Erie, Ontario L2A 5X3

Not valid to current subscribers of Harlequin Presents books.

Want to try two free books from another line?
Call 1-800-873-8635 or visit www.morefreebooks.com.

* Terms and prices subject to change without notice. N.Y. residents add applicable sales tax. Canadian residents will be charged applicable provincial taxes and GST. This offer is limited to one order per household. All orders subject to approval. Credit or debit balances in a customer's account(s) may be offset by any other outstanding balance owed by or to the customer. Please allow 4 to 6 weeks for delivery. Offer available while quantities last.

Your Privacy: Harlequin Books is committed to protecting your privacy. Our Privacy Policy is available online at www.eHarlequin.com or upon request from the Reader Service. From time to time we make our lists of customers available to reputable third parties who may have a product or service of interest to you. If you would prefer we not share your name and address, please check here. ☐

HP08

Harlequin Presents brings you
a brand-new duet by star author

Sharon Kendrick

THE GREEK BILLIONAIRES' BRIDES

Power, pride and passion—discover how only
the love and passion of two women can reunite
these wealthy, successful brothers,
divided by a bitter rivalry.

Available June 2008:

THE GREEK TYCOON'S
BABY BARGAIN

Available July 2008:

THE GREEK TYCOON'S
CONVENIENT WIFE

www.eHarlequin.com   HP12736

TALL, DARK AND SEXY

The men who never fail—seduction included!

Brooding, successful and arrogant, these men
can sweep any female they desire off her feet.
But now there's only one woman they want—
and they'll use their wealth, power, charm and
irresistibly seductive ways to claim her!

**Don't miss any of the titles in this exciting
collection available June 10, 2008:**

#9 THE BILLIONAIRE'S VIRGIN BRIDE
by **HELEN BROOKS**

#10 HIS MISTRESS BY MARRIAGE
by **LEE WILKINSON**

#11 THE BRITISH BILLIONAIRE AFFAIR
by **SUSANNE JAMES**

#12 THE MILLIONAIRE'S
MARRIAGE REVENGE
by **AMANDA BROWNING**

*Harlequin Presents EXTRA delivers a themed
collection every month featuring 4 new titles.*